HIS MOTHER'S HOUSE

<small>MARTA MORAZZONI</small> was born in Milan in 1950. She lives nearby at Gallarate, where she teaches literature in a school. Her first book, a collection of stories called *Girl in a Turban*, won international acclaim. *The Times* found it "outstanding", *Frankfurter Allgemeine* remarked on the "seamless assurance of its narrative technique" and the reviewer in *Le Monde* confessed his "unreserved admiration for a total and self-evident success".

Girl in a Turban is published in Harvill paperbacks.

by the same author

GIRL IN A TURBAN

Marta Morazzoni

HIS MOTHER'S HOUSE

Translated from the Italian by
Emma Rose

HARVILL
An Imprint of HarperCollins*Publishers*

First published with the title
Casa materna by Longanesi & C., Milan, 1992
First published in Great Britain
by Harvill
an imprint of HarperCollins*Publishers*,
77/85 Fulham Palace Road,
Hammersmith, London W6 8JB

1 3 5 7 9 8 6 4 2

A CIP record for this book
is available from the British Library.

ISBN 0 00 271254 7 (hardback)
ISBN 0 00 271380 2 (paperback)

Typeset in Linotron Garamond 3 by
Rowland Phototypesetting Ltd, Bury St Edmunds, Suffolk

Printed in Great Britain by
HarperCollins Manufacturing, Glasgow

HIS MOTHER'S HOUSE

ONE

IT HAD BEEN RAINING for days, a never-ending rain that would dwindle for an hour at most, granting the sodden city a brief respite, only to resume abruptly with renewed vigour. The lake surface, previously shrouded in a dreary thin mist, was cut into hundreds of angry gashes by these violent cloudbursts. People who had been caught out in the street, far from the shelter of the porticoes and barely protected by their raincoats and umbrellas, seemed practically annihilated by the force of the downpour.

On one of these rainy days, in a room on the first floor of a house on the edge of the lake, Mr Haakon D. was lining up five white shirts on his bed. Each had the initials H.D. embroidered in pale blue on its left-hand side – a tiny adornment, like a speck of dust in the weave of the cloth. On a coat-hanger to one side of the wardrobe hung a pair of trousers and a blue jacket, over which was laid a silk tie which had never suffered knotting. As for our gentleman's attire, for the moment it consisted of vest, underpants, bedroom slippers and socks, which were beyond reproach, pulled neatly up to his knees.

His watch informed him that he still had fifty minutes, ample time in which to catch the train for

Travemünde. Ten minutes precisely for the drive to the station, ten for getting dressed. As for packing the shirts, that would take no time at all. His razor and other toiletries were already gathered together. In a moment of uncertainty he checked to see that there really was nothing missing from the sponge-bag, then placed it in the suitcase, laid the shirts over it with great care, trying to keep them as flat as possible, and shut the case with a sharp click. Lastly, using the window as a mirror, he knotted his tie at the collar of an immaculate shirt. This was the sixth of his shirts, all of which were laundered by a daily who had the merit (as our gentleman saw it) of washing everything by hand.

Twenty minutes remained before the train's departure when Mr D. closed his front door behind him. The taxi-driver was already opening his boot in readiness for the suitcase. As the taxi proceeded in light traffic through the town centre, the traveller in the back seat mentally recited his carriage and seat numbers. He reached the station in exactly ten minutes, as he had anticipated, went in and crossed over the foot-bridge between platforms. Once down on the far platform, he immediately made for the front of the train, where his carriage would be. On the way he passed three people, two men and a woman, who were talking in animated voices – so animated, in fact, that he slowed his pace a little, his curiosity aroused by their rapid chatter, but he could make no sense of their clipped, unintelligible mutterings and so walked on, tightening his grip on the handle of his case.

At 10.02, under a driving rain which turned the world grey and drummed on the station roof, the stopping train to Travemünde moved off. Haakon D. had begun his annual journey home.

With eyes half-closed he sat for a long while, part lulled and part vexed by the swaying motion of the carriage, drifting between sleep and thought, until the train crossed a set of points at speed and he slid sideways, hitting his temple against the cold glass of the window.

Waves were lapping the beach as the train ran along the shore, while to the right the line skirted houses and gardens in the outer suburbs of Travemünde. They would shortly be entering the docks, exactly on schedule and in time for him to get a leisurely bite to eat.

Mr D. was in the habit of taking this light meal before boarding the ferry, so that later on he could remain on deck to enjoy the sight of the coastline receding and savour the prospect of an entire day of idleness, unburdened of everything, even of his physical body as it was borne upon the waters. The red towers of Oslo Town Hall would not be coming into view until noon the following day.

So it was that, two hours later, Mr D. lay stretched out on a deck chair on board ship, under a sky which was grey but promised an improvement on the Hamburg rain-clouds. Meanwhile a woman had sat down next to him, possibly the same young lady (or so he thought) that he had seen in the station at Hamburg. In his mind he called her a young lady although, judging by a quick glance, she was no longer so very young. Her skin showed signs of age and her hands on the arm-rests of the chair looked nervous, their network of veins standing out as if enduring great heat. But her reclining figure was as slim as an adolescent's, with slender hips and a flat stomach, from which he deduced she had never had children. Then he tried to forget about her, but somehow her presence disturbed him. He got up from the deck chair, pretended to look around for someone and finally moved abruptly over to the railing. The woman, for her part, gave no sign of having noticed him next to her and went on staring at the sea with her previous indifference.

Mr D. stayed away for about half an hour. When he returned, the chair next to his was empty. He stretched out peacefully at last and slipped into a state of bliss between sea and sky. Nonetheless, he still felt a vague curiosity, a languid interest in the woman, whom he did not see at dinner or even at breakfast the following morning.

As the ship entered the Oslo fjord, Mr D.'s thoughts turned to his mother, whom he had left in good health a year before and had forgotten about, so to speak, ever since. Now she was in his mind once more: the object of his journey; his sole companion for the coming month. He calculated that this was the seventeenth year of his summer homecoming: a rite performed with a punctuality worthy of both mother and son.

When the city finally opened out before him, he went down to his cabin, packed the few things he had taken out for the night, closed the suitcase and meticulously looked up the time of the Bergen train, for all that he clearly remembered everything down to the platform number. He had time to buy a newspaper and to find his seat without needing to hurry.

The journey through the mountains slipped by just as smoothly, until finally, after a few hours, the sea breeze informed him that they were approaching Bergen. On the outskirts of the city, Mr D. began to gather up his things. He worked the suitcase off the luggage-rack with short tugs, tightened up his tie and grasped his newspaper. Barely glancing at his fellow-passengers and without any discernible gesture of fare-well, he headed for the door at the end of the carriage. Few people got out at Bergen station and the train soon moved off, with a sluggish clanging.

TWO

FOR ONE DAY A YEAR, every year, time moved along a double track for Mrs Agnes D. In the glimmer of early dawn she would look out from the first-floor window of her house by the lake at Bergen, admiring the light which illuminated her garden. At the same time she would be thinking of another lake, over the sea, where her son was meticulously preparing for his departure. She would take several deep breaths at the open window before going downstairs – already fully dressed, for she hated housecoats. As a rule the drawing-room clock said eight precisely when the house began to come alive with the opening of the French windows on to the veranda and the clatter of plates in the kitchen. How different, she thought, must be the first signs of life in the Hamburg flat. At 10.02 she too heard the train echo beneath the vaulted roof of the station, and in this way, stage by stage, the 15th of June, and a large part of the following day, would unravel along parallel lines, as she waited.

Her mood was somewhere between joy and apprehension, a mildly fretful state born of the fact that she was alone for an entire year, apart from the one month of her son's visit. Not that she wasn't quite looking forward to seeing him, but between herself and the outside world — the world to which her son also belonged — she had erected an invisible barrier, forged from minute fragments of daily distrust. One could discern, behind her politely benevolent words and glances, something akin to a permanent state of alert.

Thus had she nurtured an obsessive regularity of habit: the rigid order of her hours and minutes had become a kind of tyranny, so much so that the slightest delay — even the daily's failure to present herself at the kitchen door at eight o'clock sharp — felt like a major setback. In such predicaments she would see herself as a woman standing alone against the forces of chaos, and her distant son became a mythical Knight Avenger who one day would arrive to enforce righteous order. This strange myth-making lasted only the moment of her distress, then faded away like the nervous flutter of an imperceptible muscle under an eyelid, or the glimmer of a star in the night sky. Mrs D. was perfectly content on her own.

So it was that on the morning of the 16th of June Mrs D. got up and stood at the window contemplating her garden, where the deep green of the ruffled grass merged with the sombre colour of the waves spreading from the centre of the lake. The garden was rigorously ordered and partitioned by bushes and well-pruned hedges, as Mrs D.'s love and care had dictated. Her passion for her garden had surpassed all others to the point of distancing her from other human beings. This last judgment of her, formulated by her husband in the days of what she now remembered as a stable marriage, was rather solemn, but he would pronounce it

with a touch of irony, to indicate that his deeper understanding of mankind and the world in general had
taught him to tolerate his wife's foibles and, by
accepting them, allow himself to overlook more serious
matters. Only once did the couple have a serious dis-
agreement on this subject, a dispute which was to have
significant repercussions. It was on a summer's night,
a night bathed in moonlight, that Mrs D. – looking
out from the same bedroom window she stood at now
– noticed her husband's pale silhouette (during the
summer months Mr D. liked to wear white linen),
well planted on slightly parted legs, head down, using
the bed of tea-roses as a urinal. This act, which he
would have regarded as insignificant and unprovoca-
tive, seemed to her as momentous as could be.

Years had gone by since that evening. Her husband
was dead. Yet every now and again, when she looked
at the garden from that spot, she relived the moment,
which recurred endlessly in her mind to spite her the
more, and her vexation increased with the feeling of
impotence the phantom image engendered.

Mrs D. went downstairs to prepare breakfast, mentally planning the day ahead. Her usual schedule was
to be interrupted at 5.30 in the station square. She
found it difficult to think for two people. A slight
tension coloured her most routine actions as she
reflected on the hours left to her before Haakon's arrival
and apportioned her time according to priorities,
giving pride of place to work in the garden. Two days
previously she had ordered a white azalea from the
Bergen nursery. She had had it placed, still potted, on

the lawn, in the spot that she meant to be its permanent home when it was planted out after flowering. The azalea had been delivered by the gardener's daughter, a girl of few words, with proven ability in an art which required both skill and intuition, rather like a vet's sensitivity to an animal in pain. Mrs D. had made a point of asking the young woman to return and help her at the critical stage of transplanting, when the shock to the flower would be severe.

After lunch Mrs D. took a quarter of an hour – the time she had granted herself in the morning's calculations – to smoke a leisurely cigarette before doing the washing-up. Afterwards she went to her bedroom, reckoning she could permit herself an hour and a half's sleep, after which she would dress to go into town. As a rule Mrs D. wore dark clothes, with no hint of any colour other than black and shades of grey. Her aesthetic sense advised her that if she ventured beyond these tones, vulgarity would reign.

She was already dressed when she heard, in the courtyard below, the sound of an approaching car. It was the taxi she had booked the day before to go and meet Haakon, as she did every year. She hurried downstairs, picking up her handbag and gloves from the hall table. Never, even in the middle of summer, would she have gone without her gloves: they shielded her skin from the unpleasantness of contact with objects and people. She acknowledged the driver's greeting with a brief gesture, adding only: "You know where to, don't you?"

THREE

THROUGH THE LOWERED window of the taxi
parked at the corner of the square, she saw him leave
the station, suitcase in one hand, a light panama hat
in the other. No need for false modesty – it was a
palpable, irrefutable fact: Haakon, her son, was a hand-
some man. Mrs D. had the rare good fortune not to
belong to that class of women who imprison their sons
in eternal adolescence, so that she now noted Haakon's
appearance with pleasure, a lucid eye and the feminine
awareness of any woman looking at any man.

"Mr Haakon!" The driver, standing by the open car
door, shouted and waved his cap to attract the traveller's attention as he stood looking around him. A few
moments later, sitting together on the back seat,
mother and son greeted one another without embraces
or fond words; close enough for each to make a swift,
surreptitious appraisal of the lines on the other's face,
searching for the traces another year might have etched
there.

"All well, Mother?" Haakon asked once the car had
set off and was leaving the houses of Bergen behind,
heading for the woods surrounding Lake Fantoff.

"Yes indeed, Haakon. I've no particular news . . .
nothing has changed. Life is much the same here from

one year to the next." She smiled a strange, secretive smile as she made a quick mental reckoning of the years and their uniformity.

The road left the city and for a brief moment, just before a bend, opened on to a view of the fjord.

"Oh, there is one thing," said Mrs D. "I suppose you could call it news. I've decided to let the keeper's cottage. I'm sorry I didn't consult you about it. The thing is it all happened so quickly, only a few days ago, and without my having given it much real thought. It was a chance that came up, that's all, and I thought I'd better not let it slip."

The keeper's lodge was small and quite hidden away. The narrow path which led to it came out on to the main drive, two bends before the front of the house. It was quite possible that a real lodge-keeper had never lived in it, even going back in memory to the years in which the house represented all the worldly ambitions of Haakon's grandfather, Mrs D.'s father.

As a child Haakon had played near the cottage but was forbidden to enter. Empty and isolated as it was (and as he remembered it), the lodge had nonetheless remained miraculously tidy. It seemed only right that someone should put it to good use at last and that his mother should make some money from it. He nodded without comment, gazing out of the window as the taxi turned into the driveway up to the house. His glance fell, quite involuntarily, on the path down to the cottage, and he saw no sign of change. Then the house, black and imposing, loomed towards him through the green of trees which drew apart like

17

stage-curtains. With the engine still ticking over, they unloaded Haakon's bag and, while he went up the front steps, his mother paid the driver, asking him to be so kind as to close the gates safely behind him. Mrs D. remained outside for a moment, followed the sound of the car retreating down the hill, heard the clang of the gates then, satisfied as the roar of acceleration dwindled into the distance, she too climbed the three steps up to the house.

She joined her son in the darkened hallway where he had been waiting for her and led the way into the drawing-room, where the curtains were tightly drawn, as the mistress of the house feared the effects of sunlight.

She left him alone for a minute, confronted with the curious sensation of returning to a house which had been his home, where the memory of some former familiarity − if not that familiarity itself − had been lying dormant and was reawakened by touching an object, seeing the way a shadow fell in a corner or light filtered through a crack: the same light as in years gone by. Every time he came back Haakon experienced this same bewilderment, counteracted by his mother's briskness and efficiency. Indeed it was she who picked up the suitcase he had abandoned in the middle of the room and, driven by her anxiety for order, was even about to start struggling up the stairs with it, at which Haakon hastened to her side and relieved her of her burden.

Together they entered the bedroom that had been his as a boy. It still had the same light wooden furniture, the same wine-coloured bedspread, too sombre for a child. His mother's welcome was conspicuous in everything: in the impeccable way the sheets were ironed, in the spotless towels and in the expression with which she now inspected the room, searching for the slightest imperfection, a crooked fold in the curtains or a chair out of position.

"I'll make some tea," she said. "I imagine you'll be wanting something to eat as well." She left him alone to arrange his few things in the cupboard. When the door closed Haakon stood motionless for a moment, hesitant, then with a mechanical movement pulled open a drawer in the chest under the window to look over and touch the old boyhood sweaters he still wore when he was here.

From the window he could see the garden sloping down towards the lake, where the full afternoon sun made metallic flashes on the surface of the water. Not a single breath of air to stir the tops of the trees. From the floor below came the clatter of crockery en route from kitchen to dining-room. Later on, well into the night, these sounds would be heard again as his mother restored the house to order after dinner. And then, out of the silence of the lake and the shadows of the night, the house would emerge like an island, blacker than the darkness.

FOUR

THE NEXT MORNING as he lay half asleep, this bed in his childhood room became confused in his mind with the one at home in Hamburg. Turning on to his side, he expected to see the usual bare white wall, but was disorientated by the colours of an unknown wallpaper. It was only a matter of seconds before his awakened mind recovered the remembrance of familiarity; before his body, for its part, rediscovered the accustomed route between bed and window – a straight line, free of obstacles. He opened the curtains, forcing himself to brave the light which assailed him, and leaned out to look into the garden, from which rose an indistinct chatter of voices. There he saw his mother in a daring outfit such as only she would have risked, and then only in the privacy of her own home: a pair of her husband's old trousers, turned up at the ankles and belted at the waist over a white blouse with the sleeves rolled up; and it was remarkable how, on that frame burdened by the years, this inelegant combination acquired such an air of austerity. Kneeling down beside Mrs D., practically on all fours, was a young woman he had never seen before. His slight shortsightedness did not prevent him from recognising his mother's figure, but as for the other woman, all he could make out were a few features: black hair and the general impression of a sturdy physique.

Down in the kitchen to heat up the coffeepot, he heard their voices more distinctly: the young woman's was low-pitched and resonant. He caught something about bedding out a plant and their discussion, with their alternating tones of voice, was a lively one. He paid little attention, never having been one for botany. He saw to his own needs and, having finished his breakfast, lingered in the dining-room looking through the old newspapers his mother kept neatly stacked on the chest of drawers, next to the radio.

"Come in and wash your hands, Felice. Would you like some tea, or a glass of milk? It's such a hot morning!" Mrs D. came in from garden, followed by a girl whose hands were covered in earth; she was holding her outstretched fingers well away from her dress as if they did not belong to her. Neither of them seemed to notice Haakon sitting motionless in an armchair, watching them. They passed close by him and went into the corridor, heading for the kitchen. From there, muffled by the sound of running water, their voices failed to reach him, so he stood up and wandered slowly out into the garden. He stopped by the freshly dug and recently watered hole, where a white azalea with a few surviving flowers had just been planted facing towards the lake and well-sheltered by a box hedge.

"All in all, this is the mildest spot." Haakon was startled by the sound of his mother's voice behind him. Moving across the lawn in her plush slippers she was as silent and light as a shadow. Even as a boy Haakon had harboured a vague fear of being attacked from behind; so much so that at times, alone in his Hamburg flat, he would feel compelled – though afraid – to wheel round and catch some presence behind his back, whether a man or a shade.

Standing beside him now, regarding the little plant sternly, she said:

"For the first few months it is bound to suffer. According to Felice it will lose a lot of leaves. But if it can just manage to take root, it will have plenty of shelter here all through the winter." She was talking to herself, Haakon realised, and, as she talked, she was already nursing the azalea with her eyes, betraying a Spartan tenderness.

"Who is Felice?" he asked.

"Didn't you see her? She was with me in the garden a little while ago. I thought I had told you about her anyway. She's the daughter of the gardener in Bergen and a great help to her father."

"No, I don't recall you mentioning her before."

Mrs D. thought for a moment, then remembered: "I've only been dealing with her since last spring, before then it was her father who came up here. She's an excellent woman. Most thorough." She bent down to pat the ground with her fingertips and Haakon left her there, ministering to the plant as gently and anxiously as someone tucking in an invalid. He walked towards the lake, all the way to the shore, along a path which sloped gently downwards and ended at the water's edge beside a stone bench lapped by the waves. As a little boy he used to lie down on this bench,

facing out towards the lake with the feeling of being
a castaway, and would clutch at the stone rim of the
seat with desperate strength, as if it really were a matter
of life and death. As he grew older the game could no
longer be kept up: the opposite shore was actually quite
close, the bench too short to stretch out on, so the
dream of being shipwrecked turned to nothing. For all
that, his languid pleasure in the lapping of the waves
did not diminish.

He sat on the ground and watched the slow un-
dulation of the lake, the pummelling of the little waves
raising and releasing the muddy bottom close to the
shore, like the pumping of a heart or lungs breathing
long and deep.

He spent what was left of the morning in idleness,
without even summoning the curiosity to turn his head
towards the house, content with the monotony of the
lake, the cool of the grass and the heat of the sun
beating down on nearby stone. He thought about
the days ahead, made plans to fish in the fjord, go
for walks, even give his mother a hand in the garden.
A whole month stretched before him, calm and
untroubled as the surface of the lake. The opposite
shore was close, only a few strokes away for a strong
swimmer, and he thought of crossing to the other side
one day – one of the thirty days to come.

FIVE

TWO DAYS AFTER the transplanting of the azalea, Mrs D. rang Felice. Making telephone calls was not something she did willingly, even though she was used to the instrument, which her husband had been one of the first in the district to have installed, shortly after their marriage. The intrusiveness of the telephone annoyed her; even worse was the inability to see the other person's face, particularly when it was somebody of importance to her. Despite all this, she had Felice summoned to the telephone at her father's plant-nursery in town. It was early morning and Haakon, who had just left on one of his long walks, would not be back until lunch-time. The morning was exceptionally beautiful and the garden, in all its summer splendour, seemed to be pleading for the gift of new plants. Standing on the veranda outside the kitchen, her cup of coffee still in her hand, Mrs D. looked around her and felt pleased with herself and a little moved.

So Felice was summoned for consultation and asked to come up to the house.

"Bring some rhododendron plants with you. They grow in the wild and they're hardier than roses. Three of my young rose plants died last winter, the white ones in the middle of the beds," Mrs D. complained

24

over the telephone, and on the other end of the line the girl agreed that this was the right time to be planting rhododendrons.

"Excellent. In that case, Felice, come whenever you want to. Any time would suit me. Today would be perfect. Right away if you like."

The girl went up to the house on one of the earliest trams from the station, carrying her precious burden with care. There were few passengers at that hour, so she made herself comfortable and concentrated on looking out for the stop near the house. She had made the journey so often of late that she knew the route well, but remained watchful out of a sheer mania for punctuality. She rang the bell at the gate but, without waiting for an answer, opened it herself and entered the drive, making her way up the slope that led to the house. The tall trees on either side of the road resembled the fringes of a wood, and concealed the presence of the house at the top of the hill.

Rounding a bend, Felice saw Mrs D. waiting for her, standing stock-still at the end of the drive. She took no step towards Felice, gave no hint of a smile of welcome. Mrs D. was not well liked in town: everybody knew it, including herself. Too haughty to yield to the slightest intimacy, she was presumed to be happy in her isolation. It was said that only an eccentric like Felice – herself such a solitary character – could get through to Mrs D., by means of the only affection that elderly lady had ever displayed: her loving pride in her garden.

A short while later the two were busily seeking out

the best site for the rhododendron bushes, and the older woman was meekly acquiescing to the judgment of the younger.

"Look, this is the most sheltered spot, even in the worst of winters. And then if you wanted, this year while the plants are still young, you could build a windbreak to the north of them. It's easy – I could make it myself out of wood or bamboo. All you need is a screen." Felice indicated the position and the required height. Together they worked at planting out the shrubs and midday arrived without anything having distracted them.

Haakon returned when the clock had just struck one and found them hard at work. The hem of his mother's skirt was muddied and the young woman was using her hands to firm in the recently dug flower-bed round the base of one of the rhododendrons. He drew closer to them and watched quietly for a few moments, unobserved. It was Felice who saw him first. She cast a stern glance in his direction, nodded, and went on working round the plant. But his mother chose to introduce him to the young woman as solemnly as if they had been at a formal dinner.

"Felice, allow me to present my son Haakon. I don't believe you have met." Haakon bowed slightly to acknowledge the ceremoniousness of their meeting, but did not join in the conversation between the two women. He only noted, with surprise, how Miss Felice held his mother's attention to the exclusion of all else.

"Well, Madam," said Felice, dusting off her dress and rubbing the earth from her hands as she got up,

"I have to get back to Bergen now. The tram comes by in ten minutes."

"Why don't you stay to lunch with us, Felice?"

At this, Haakon started slightly and shot a worried, furtive glance towards his mother and the girl. Felice declined firmly, without offering any explanation beyond a simple "No, thank you," nor did Mrs D. attempt to persuade her, but led her to the laundry-room to tidy herself up, leaving Haakon standing alone in front of the young plant with its pale-green leaves.

Soon afterwards he caught sight of Felice striding off down the hill at a brisk pace, never looking back. He took a few steps in the same direction just in time to observe her purposeful stride, the suppleness of her hips and the natural grace of her movements, before Felice disappeared round the last bend in the drive.

A moment later the gates shut with a clang, almost in unison with the rattle of the tram.

SIX

AT MEALTIMES MOTHER and son sat opposite each other, each in the same place, always. Haakon's was a legacy from his father, the recognised and consecrated seat of the head of the family, according to the long-established rules of the house which in seemingly trivial details were as rigid as the Ten Commandments and were, like them, graven in the hearts of the household. At the first dinner after the old gentleman's funeral, in a sort of tacit investiture ceremony, his son had occupied that chair, which had stood empty ever since Mr D.'s worsening illness had confined him to his bed on the first floor. Haakon was not even twenty-one when he had come into that legacy yet he could remember as though it were yesterday his mother's grave look and her gesture of assent qualified by a stab of melancholy. That was all. Not a word passed between them on the subject.

In any case, after the old gentleman's death, the dining-table gradually lost its importance in the household. Mrs D. had no particular aptitude for cookery and was not fond of devoting time in the kitchen to the exercise of her culinary imagination. The meals she prepared for her son combined the virtue of simplicity with the vice of monotony, but Haakon had never complained. Ever since he had been coming back only once a year, and for a relatively short stay, he had begun to notice how a strict ceremonial always accompanied the serving of exactly the same dishes, or rather the same dish for every day of the week. It was all so methodical that, to the question: "What is for lunch?" it would have been sufficient to reply: "It's Wednesday" (and so without the shadow of a doubt it would be poached salmon). But precisely because Haakon's visits to his mother's house had been reduced to that one month, he found that this repetition, far from irking him, provided a bridge to link one year to the next with the comfort of continuity. So Wednesday was poached salmon, the dish which Felice would have shared with them had she accepted the invitation.

In contrast to the simplicity of the menu, the table had been laid with great care, with no stinting on fine china and crystal or indeed the silver, which seemed to be in everyday use. Haakon could not have said (nor, for that matter, had he ever asked), whether this was also the case during the months when his mother sat down to meals alone. Certainly when he was there the table setting never betrayed the slightest oversight.

Picture Felice at that table! Wouldn't a girl who was probably unused to such luxury have felt flustered? Haakon wondered about this but did not voice the question until it slipped out almost by accident in the murmured remark: "Wouldn't it have been a little embarrassing for her, and for us too come to that, if she had stayed to lunch?"

His mother gave him a withering look; her words brooked no contradiction: "I cannot imagine Felice being daunted by anything." She tempered this with a half-smile. Haakon handled the heavy silver with ease, slicing the fish into small pieces which he then matched, one at a time, on his fork with similar pieces of boiled potato, and chewed slowly.

"You seem to have a very high opinion of this . . . this girl of yours."

"Just because I don't believe she would be embarrassed by a family lunch? There are far better reasons than that for me to think highly of her. If that is what you meant . . ." she answered. Then her smile widened, to soften the observation that rose spontaneously to her lips: "I can't help wondering if perhaps it isn't a case of *her* making *you* feel a trifle awkward, my dear."

Haakon did not reply. The light from the window overlooking the garden was changing and the sun giving way to an unsettled mass of clouds. The first thing to darken was the water of the lake. He got up as soon as the meal was over, pushed his chair in and said, with a slight bow:

"That was excellent, as always. Now I am going to go and have a look outside. The weather seems to be changing."

The moment her son had gone out of the veranda doors, Mrs D. got up too, cleared the table with a few deft movements and quickly put the room back into perfect order. A recent row with the latest daily help had left her with a feeling of great energy, at least in these early days, and a proud need for self-sufficiency.

Haakon and his mother did not meet for the whole of that afternoon, although he was aware of her presence in the house by various signs. The meal that brought them together that evening did not inspire anything more than casual conversation: trivial remarks made in expressionless voices, calculated not to make contact with each other in any way. Mostly they spoke of the next day and what it would bring. Then, as if imparting some casual piece of information, Mrs D. said:

"Tomorrow, Haakon, we will not be seeing each other until lunch. In fact – I promise it won't happen again, it is an exceptional circumstance – I may have to ask you to wait an extra half-hour for lunch, to give me time to get back from Bergen."

"Do you need me to come with you? Can I be of any assistance?"

"No, no, you must feel free to do whatever you like tomorrow. I would never dream of . . . besides I can deal with the matter perfectly well on my own. It's the tenancy agreement for the cottage – it just needs my signature and a final adjustment to the rent. But basically it is settled and all quite straightforward. I manage quite well on my own, believe me."

They said goodnight. Mrs D. stayed on at the table adding up figures in an exercise book, and Haakon went upstairs with a bundle of newspapers under his arm. Once in his room, he put them down on the chest of drawers under the window and looked out at the sky, which was still bright, though traversed by heavy, rain-laden clouds. The mass of the lake was the colour of lead and the last daylight overshadowed by the imminent downpour.

SEVEN

PERHAPS AT THIRTY-FIVE or so, perhaps later, when he was approaching his forties: he himself could not have said at what age his insomnia had begun. It was not real insomnia at first, just an occasional, insignificant delay in falling asleep – a slight divergence between his body and his mind, which continued to wander lucidly through the night shadows. Sooner or later though, fatigue would gain the upper hand, imposing the silence of sleep – he had only to be patient, to allow his nerves to slacken one by one, like bowstrings at rest. As time went on this was not always the case, indeed it became less and less so; his heart would start beating furiously against his ribs and his worry over the day which had ended overlapped with his anxiety for the day which was to come, leaving him no respite. Since untroubled sleep had been a feature of his youth, this insomnia had to represent a transition into a new stage of his life, a slow and ominous metamorphosis; initially just a surface scratch on a smooth piece of slate, but then a deeper mark, carved out. Only in the house at Bergen did it never happen, perhaps because the walls were so very familiar; because he felt so safe in his old room, where nothing had changed since his adolescence and every object

33

conspired with him to loosen the knots of his anxiety.

He moved away from the window, took a longer pull on his cigarette, then another, then stubbed it out – otherwise, in the morning, his mother would scold him for the stale smell of tobacco in the room. Perhaps it was the half-light which had descended on the garden and the dark clouds obscuring the sky that made him feel strangely apprehensive. From where he stood he could still distinguish through the dusk the white blur of the azalea, giving off a milky luminescence. He turned away and went over to sit on the bed – reluctantly, because he could feel, growing and congealing within him, an insidious fear of the night; a dread of being overpowered by it. Possibly this was all more imagined than real, more a discomfort than a pain; in any case there was nothing for it but to pull himself together and confront what was to come. More than once it had occurred to him that it might be easier to bear the weight of the unknown if he were not alone. On such occasions, eschewing human companionship, he would think of an animal, a dog curled up in dreamless sleep at the foot of the bed, who could be awakened by the slightest movement, or by a single light pat on the head, to share its master's unease. Surrounded by the complete silence which hung over house, garden and lake, he was struck by the awful thought that death might be an endless night without sleep.

He heard his mother's heavy footsteps on the stairs. A shaft of light from the lamp in the corridor appeared under his bedroom door. Then, a moment before he

heard the metallic click of a door closing, darkness
fell.

His mother and father had been married fifty years
earlier, in the black church of a remote village in the
province of Ål. There was no more than a handful of
guests yet the church was so small that there was only
room for some of them. The rest waited outside, chat-
ting as they strolled around the churchyard and looking
from time to time towards the storiated church door,
closed at present, on whose threshold the newly-weds
would appear. Even though many years had passed,
Mrs D. was still moved by the memory of her wedding
day – after the service, before the couple left the
church, her husband had taken the bouquet from her
hands and leant down to place it on the tomb of the
Archbishop of Stavanger.

Haakon had never seen the village, the church,
or the grave of the prelate from across the sea who
had gone to die there so long ago, in a village at
the foot of the mountain, and who now lay enclosed
within the wooden walls of this diminutive church.
But ever since childhood, listening to his mother's
account, he had constructed in his mind that little
church of dark wood: its doorway decorated like the
prow of an ancient ship and, inside it, the tomb: a
vast and solemn structure which by some miracle of
proportions managed to fit into the building. This
miracle persisted in Haakon's adult mind – for him,
even now, the sepulchre towered solemnly in the nave
of a cathedral, where, larger still, loomed the white

35

figure of his father (in his linen summer clothes, as the child had often seen him), stooping to place his bride's flowers on the tomb.

EIGHT

MRS D. ROSE EARLY the next morning. It was a rainy day: the lawn glistened greener from the drops of a light shower, so light that it gave the impression of leaving the shrubs and flowers at rest beneath a glossy, refreshing cover of organza. She went down the stairs, taking care not to make the least noise that might disturb her son. In the sitting-room she unearthed the old tram timetable from a drawer crammed with papers, consulted it, put it away again after re-folding it along its creases, then busied herself so as to be ready in time.

Mrs D. was at the gate five minutes early, waiting for the tram which, in a journey of less than twenty minutes, would take her to Bergen station. From there she made for the old quarter which lay at the foot of the mountain, squeezed between the green slopes and the sea. She paused for a moment at a fork in the street, then turned left, following a labyrinthine route among small houses, narrow doorways and streets whose cobbles were worn by the tread of everyday comings and goings. She found the house, which had no bell or knocker on its door, so that she had to rap vigorously with her knuckles. She instinctively took a step back when a sound from within warned her that someone was coming.

An hour later she came out, with the relieved and confident air of one who has just dispelled a doubt. Walking faster and with a lighter step, she took a longer route back to the station, emerging from the old quarter next to the small lake which was overlooked by a row of Bergen's prosperous middle-class villas. In spite of the persistent rain, which was actually heavier than before, she walked by the lake for quite a while, keeping close to the edge, enjoying the play of water on water, and herself toying with the handle of her umbrella – twirling it gently between her fingers so that a crown of droplets swirled around her head. It was only a matter of seconds before Mrs D. recovered her composure and her usual sedate demeanour then, with studied leisureliness, set off again for the station. Once there, she sat for nearly ten minutes alone in a stationary tram, waiting for it to leave the terminus. As this was the midday service, things only began to get busy a few minutes before the hour struck, when the tram filled up with an assortment of faces, mostly male, talking loudly, occupying every available space and deafening her with their boisterousness. Mrs D., who had now regained her customary gravity, briefly considered how men's adolescent temperament in-variably surfaced at the very slightest provocation. She herself had never seen the attraction of adolescence; she remembered her own only reluctantly, and had disliked her son's even more, short though it had been. Haakon, she seemed to remember, had got over it very quickly.

She arrived home before the end of the half-hour's leeway she had agreed with her son, so lunch was not late.

"I've tried to lay the table," said Haakon, greeting her full of eagerness to help, "but there's bound to be something missing."

Mrs D. was in good humour. She glanced quickly over the dining-table, nodded her approval and, with unwonted levity, added: "On the contrary, hardly anything is missing — if we don't consider cutlery as essential, that is . . ." She realised she had disconcerted Haakon by adopting a jovial manner which was not customary between the two of them, and she decided not to proceed further into the convolutions of an unpredictable game, beyond the bounds of their rules. She hurried upstairs to put away her overcoat and bag and to change into her indoor clothes. Then she went back down to prepare bread, butter and herrings, their ritual fare on Thursdays, when, by a habit acquired during the years when her husband went out to work, their main meal was taken in the evening.

Over lunch they made light conversation, chiefly about the weather. It was not until afterwards, when Haakon was already ensconced in an armchair with his newspaper, that he began to feel an idle curiosity about the fate of the keeper's cottage.

"Who is the tenant going to be?" he asked, and his mother replied: "Felice."

Haakon's short sight was always at its worst when he needed to shift his glance rapidly from a nearby object to a distant one. It took him a long time to focus. So when he raised his eyes from the newspaper, he was unable to decipher his mother's expression with any certainty. He should have given himself time; he should have looked at her for a moment longer until he could see her clearly. But it was not Haakon's habit to hold anybody's gaze.

NINE

"OW OLD ARE YOU going to be on your next birthday, Haakon? Forty-seven?"

It was five o'clock on the first sunny afternoon after three days of heavy rain. Mother and son were sitting in the drawing-room by the veranda, drinking tea. At Mrs D.'s question, Haakon raised his eyes from his cup and stared at her in amazement, then turned towards the open window with its view of the lake. His only reply was a nod.

After a moment's silence Mrs D. spoke again, pursuing her own train of thought: "I suppose by now you no longer think about getting . . . about matrimony?" she said, and added hurriedly: "No, no, believe me, I've no wish to pry into matters that do not concern me."

For eleven months out of twelve over the past seventeen years, her son's whole life had been a matter that did not concern her. It had never occurred to her to board a ship bound for the continent and to visit the city where he led a life of which she knew very little; only a few scattered details. She had seen a photograph of the building the address of which Haakon had sent her years ago. Quite a high-class place, it looked. Haakon, for his part, had never actually invited her.

"After all, you are happy in Hamburg. It is the right sort of city for someone of your temperament."

"Well, I've got used to it over the last seventeen years, at any rate," Haakon replied eventually, in the light, detached tone of a casual remark. As for her insinuation about marriage, he completely ignored it.

"When you left home for the first time you were the same age as Felice is now. She is thirty." Mrs D. said. The new tenant's name had not been mentioned for the past three days, and the rain had prevented her from visiting the garden.

"So your garden is in such dire need of attention that you decided to induce her to live here . . ." Haakon's voice sought to be free of all emotion or inflection, but his gaze, shifting restlessly around the room — unable to settle even on the unbroken calm of the lake at the end of the lawn — betrayed a measure of unease.

Mrs D. shook some crumbs off the hem of her skirt, then leant over the tray in search of another slice of bread — not too large or too heavily buttered — picked one up in her fingertips, held it in front of her, examining it out of the corner of her eye, then at last replied:

"My dear Haakon, I really do not think I have induced anyone to do anything. My garden, as you well know, is very important to me, but I can still look after it on my own, as long as my strength allows . . . All the same, the idea of having some assistance is not unwelcome, though that takes second place to other considerations. And yet . . . " She paused for a moment to look at him. "And yet, maybe in all this there is something that displeases you . . . Or perhaps upsets you?"

In certain predicaments his mother's insight was embarrassing. "Other considerations", she had said, and to Haakon this seemed to conceal, to imply, some long-meditated strategy. It was true that, in the seventeen years which separated him from this newcomer, Felice, his world had revolved around one point, a static invariable. But possibly he had failed to notice that over that time, something had made a movement imperceptible to the naked eye. Observed every day, a crack in the wall remains at the same height, seemingly motionless – yet one day you find it has suddenly extended upwards. Thus for years, never deviating from the path of the most entrenched habit, Haakon had thought that only a chance event could effect any change – an event such as death. But it seemed to him that the crossroads now before him had not been arrived at by chance, and deep in his heart, in the place where reason had no voice, Haakon felt himself to be floundering breathlessly. He looked around him, and nothing had been moved from its place, not even an ornament; the smell of the house – his mother's smell – was the same as ever. He reflected that for years we can walk, blithe and unthinking, on the brink of certain chasms, until one day we stumble, even slightly, and are forced to look down into the depths.

His mother was waiting for a response to her question, her silence spurring him to speak.

"Upsets me? Not at all," Haakon lied. "Why should it upset me?" he went on, lying more convincingly, and finally pausing to look at his mother's face – at her tanned skin and her clear eyes surrounded by wrinkles. She, for her part, calmly returned his gaze.

"This year I shall be seventy and I don't feel the weight of my years. That is why I allow myself not to conceal my age from anyone." She chose a third slice of bread with the same care as before, put it on her plate and poured tea for herself and her son, without asking him if he wanted more. The dark liquid sat untouched in the pearly china teacup. Haakon did not take so much as a sip. He rose, leaving the conversation in mid-air together with all the reflections that were beginning to come to light. He turned from his mother to look at the garden through the French windows of the veranda, then walked out, descended the few steps, and approached the azalea, his hands in his pockets. The young plant had lost all its flowers; its clean, shiny leaves spread themselves in the sunlight. The surface of the lake shone too, and at the water's edge the castaway-stone, the seat he had played on as a child, was absorbing the heat, making up for the dampness of the past few days. Haakon went to sit down, imagining that the mere act of touching stone with his bare hands and feeling it through his clothes would allow him to recapture the calm to which he had surrendered that first day, not even a week ago. Or rather, *already* nearly a week ago – which meant he had only three weeks left.

TEN

HAAKON HAD BEEN little more than a child — if he remembered rightly it was in the summer of his tenth year, a beautiful, hot summer — when his father had decided to take him along on one of the usually solitary expeditions he had been treating himself to more and more frequently. Sometimes Mr D. would be away from home for whole days at a stretch, having left his wife with only a rough idea of where he was going. For Haakon it was an honour to be invited to take part in such an expedition — both an honour and an embarrassment. Would he rise to the challenge, without being a nuisance to his father? Would they be back after one day? After two? Where would they sleep? These were questions that could not be asked, but in the child's mind the pleasure of adventure was weakened by the uncertainty, by the desire to be reassured, by the fear of missing his own bed and his own room, and by a shudder that ran through him at the prospect of the distance and of the unknown. He did not refuse, but left with a heavy heart.

The train took them south from Bergen to Stavanger — a seemingly endless journey. At Stavanger, right outside the station, a bus with a handful of passengers aboard was waiting for their train. It took them inland, along roads that all merged together in the child's mind; steep roads that climbed endlessly upwards. And their destination, when they reached it, turned out to be the start of an utterly abandoned path, which they ventured up alone as the bus drove on heaven knows where, raising a cloud of dust that made their eyes smart. Far below them, still in the distance, Haakon spotted the waters of a fjord or lake that ran parallel to the first stage of their climb. The path was rugged; a stone track which soon entered a wood of pine and chestnut trees where the earth beneath their feet felt softer under its carpet of leaves and pine needles. They emerged into a bright green, swampy meadow and were forced to make their way along a line of planks which Haakon could see bending under his father's weight.

Then they were back on the stony ground, very steep now and without even the trace of a path.

"Walk in my footsteps," his father said, turning to see how the child was getting on. Deep in his heart Haakon was wavering between fear and the desire not to disappoint or hinder his guide. The ground made hard walking and the day was unsettled by the frequent scudding of clouds which cast dark shadows on to the stones. And the stones grew and grew, until they were no longer even stones but boulders that Haakon set his foot on gingerly, with the sensation of stepping on grey, menacing islands.

"Want to stop?" his father asked, when they had been walking for more than an hour, and Haakon only had enough breath for a vigorous shake of the head, signalling a "no" which he would not have had the strength to voice. They went on, frighteningly alone, among mountains taller than any he had ever seen at Bergen. Walking along the ridge of a large boulder and looking past a jutting wedge of rock, he glimpsed the distant segment of an unattainable fjord; but then, a few steps further on, it disappeared from view.

The grey rock walls now contrasted with a sky which had been swept clear of clouds, and the sun shone bright on the boulders. Time passed – half an hour or more – then the water reappeared in the distance; a great, glittering, deep inlet between the towering cliffs. Haakon told himself they were trying to reach a mirage. He kept his gaze on it, convinced that if he looked away it would vanish once more, this time forever.

He lost all heart when a sudden turn in the path hid the water from view and plunged the two wayfarers back among the mountains. Finally in front of them rose a smooth wall of rock with no footholds. To the left of the small area of level, mossy ground they were standing on, a path forced its way between the high cliff and a lesser one, and Mr D. set off along this track, motioning to the child to stay close behind him and to walk carefully. The path emerged into the open and for the space of a yard or less overlooked a yawning chasm, a sheer drop down to the Liesefjord. Haakon clung to the rock-face and his sweating hand left a dark print on the grey surface of the stone. They reached a narrow ledge, a few yards long and sheltered at the back by the cliff they had just rounded.

They were on a natural balcony above the fjord. His father went to the very edge, lay down on his stomach and, gripping the stone ledge, stretched his head out into the void. Once he had scrambled to his knees, then to his feet, he cast a stern look at his son. His eyes shone with a strange light.

"Look down there, Haakon," he said. "Don't be afraid, I'll hold you by the ankles."

As the child knelt down and, with bated breath, stretched out towards the abyss, he felt his father's hands grip his ankles like a vice. Only then did he open his eyes wide on the fjord spread out beneath him, violet and infinite in the silence.

Night after night thereafter, as his limbs first started growing heavy with drowsiness, and later, in the depths of sleep, those colours and that silence again took possession of him, at once a dream and a nightmare in the mind and eyes of the child.

He dreamt of it again that Saturday night, just as he had in his childhood. He felt the vice-like grip of his father's hands on his ankles, but the water and the rocks below were enveloped in a dazzling swathe of milk-white mist.

He had trouble waking up and it was very late; a strange unease sapped his will to get out of bed, so he lingered there, examining himself limb by limb, yet could find nothing wrong anywhere. It was not even nausea, this discomfort that ran through his every fibre. He forced himself to get up and disregard the oppressive sensation, but the few steps he took left him totally exhausted, like a doddering old man who finds every movement an effort. He ran his hands through the thinning hair at his temples, and sank into the armchair by the window, keeping his eyes tightly shut lest the panes reflect an unpleasant image of his condition.

They were both in the garden, his mother and Felice. He could hear their voices clearly: his mother's lively and animated, Felice's placid and imperturbable. Haakon felt a pang of revulsion, of overwhelming disgust, and thus he remained for perhaps half an hour, during which time the voices outside only reached him as a jumble of meaningless sounds.

Sleep returned unnoticed, and the white mist of the fjord rose up once more, impelling him yet again to strive to break through and reach the brilliant violet of the water.

He did not go downstairs until just before midday, by which time he had completely regained his self-possession. Smelling fresh from his recent shave, he was impeccably dressed, and showed no trace of that morning's malaise. Felice had already returned to her father's plant-nursery in town, and Haakon's mother was sitting in the drawing-room reading a newspaper, something which she could still manage without spectacles. She looked up at her son with a smile — the same smile that had been lighting up her face before she noticed Haakon's presence in the room.

ELEVEN

THREE DAYS LATER, in the middle of the week, Felice was to move in. Haakon only learned about this by chance, and felt unsure whether to attribute his mother's silence on the subject to her thoughtfulness; to her reluctance to involve him unnecessarily; or was he not perhaps being deliberately excluded from proceedings in which he was not meant to interfere? But seeing that he had found out, he thought it best to mention his willingness to help as best he could. Haakon was not a man blessed with great practical ability and the recollection of his awkwardness brought an ironic gleam to Mrs D.'s eye, although she put on a show of appreciating the generosity of the offer. She thanked him. If it became necessary she would call on him, but only if it did not interfere with his plans for the day, which he must not alter on any account. "On *any* account," she repeated firmly.

Haakon listened as they sat in the drawing-room after dinner, in the amber light of the evening. The move was to take place the following morning. The crescendo of precautions and reservations expressed by his mother, and her concern not to put him to any trouble, fermented in him a vague but growing irritability that turned to self-recrimination. It nettled him not to understand what his role should be in this matter or what was the right thing to do. Should he go away for half the day and keep out of the whole business, or should he stay at home? And if he did stay, how could he tell whether he was wanted or not?

He stayed. In the morning he was in the kitchen unusually early, listening out for the sound of the cart on the cobbled surface of the drive. Also waiting was Mrs D., who had put on her gardening clothes in order to be comfortable as she worked.

"It's a bit strange, don't you think, for the lady of the house to assist so . . . so fully when a tenant moves in?" Haakon asked. Mrs D. was sitting opposite her son smoking a leisurely cigarette, so deep in thought that she appeared not to have heard a thing: her only response was a vacant glance. As for Haakon, he was feeling rather put out by all this fuss over something in which he did not really have a part; almost as if he had stumbled absentmindedly into a bramble-bush and grazed his arms. They heard the gate open, then the sound of hooves and a heavy cart on the cobblestones.

Haakon wondered whether Felice had accompanied the gardener's boy; whether she too would be perched amongst all the furniture stacked on the cart. He immediately followed his mother, who had carefully extinguished her cigarette and emptied the ashtray so as not to foul the air with stale smoke. As she led the way out by the back door, Mrs D. gave him one last glance, saying: "Honestly Haakon, there's no need . . ." He compressed his lips slightly, then dismissed the matter with a wave of the hand. They walked to the

51

top of the slope and stopped in the middle of the drive. By the path to the cottage stood the cart – fairly empty, as it turned out. It had been driven there by a young man with whom Felice seemed to be on very familiar terms – the "boy", of course. Standing at his side, she was looking up at the pile of things, absorbed in mental calculations as to how, and in what order, they should unload the furniture and fittings, where they should all be put and how to get them down the path to the keeper's lodge.

Mrs D. approached Felice and, with unaccustomed cordiality, placed a hand on her arm and talked to her briefly. Then, turning towards Haakon, she said:

"My son has offered to help. I'm sure it won't take long. And I'm certain," she added, turning back to the young woman, "that you have more experience of this sort of thing than we do, because we really have very little." She was smiling – enjoying herself, Haakon thought. In no time they decided how to proceed, and it was in fact the two women who took charge. Both displayed exemplary energy and practicality; they seldom spoke, saying only what was necessary to complete the task. Haakon found himself doing precisely what Felice, polite and firm, asked of him, while she in turn carried chairs and other objects. It was Felice who helped him lift the heavy table-top and Haakon, who had been expecting to take most of the weight, was struck by the young woman's virile strength.

It was midday by the time the empty cart was ready to return to Bergen. Before she climbed on to the box beside the young man, who had already taken up the reins, Felice paused to stroke the nose of the horse, which had patiently borne all the comings and goings and the jolts of the unloading. Then she turned to Haakon with a stern look and thanked him for his help, adding,

"Please tell your mother I will be back this afternoon, to work in the garden."

At the bottom of the drive Felice got down to open the gate, then shut it again with ease, lifting it slightly where a raised cobble prevented it from swinging smoothly. She climbed back on to the cart without looking towards Haakon, who was watching her from the top of the drive. He noticed how comfortable she seemed with her surroundings, as if the house had been hers for a long while. Then he went inside to join his mother, who had already been preparing lunch for some time.

TWELVE

HE CAME THAT afternoon as promised, but did not set foot in the keeper's cottage; gardening engaged all her attention. From the veranda Haakon once again observed the complicity between the two women, which expressed itself in the way their movements harmonised, and in their brief exchanges, of which he caught only a few words. They worked on until late afternoon. After that Felice did not re-appear for some days.

To Haakon the old keeper's lodge seemed more desolate than ever now that it had been invaded by alien furniture, haphazardly placed. More than once he found himself wandering around outside it, even venturing to the back window to peer through the glass and spy on what little was visible: only the silhouettes of the furniture – that same pile of household objects which he had helped carry from the cart. The cottage was shrouded in darkness by the trees, both sheltered and stifled by vegetation which nobody had cut back for years.

"Your tenant seems to have mistaken the cottage for an old furniture store," he finally commented one Sunday evening, as he sat in the drawing-room with his mother. He tried to adopt a tone of benevolent irony and to betray no real curiosity, but his voice came out tinged with bitterness.

Mrs D., on the other hand, replied calmly, saying that Felice had, after all, signed the contract, had observed its terms and paid the advance, and therefore had the right to do whatever she liked with the cottage, even not live there at all.

"Of course, yes, you're right," Haakon said, retreating instantly. "I wouldn't want you to think I was interfering in something which has nothing to do with me. Nothing to do with me at all," he repeated. "I'm leaving in two weeks and for a least a year I'll have no part in all this. Even now I am not involved in your decision, or in hers, I realise that. I was giving an opinion, nothing more." He was expecting a reply which never came. His mother was concentrating intently on some sewing – a task for which she had never shown any aptitude – and appeared not to hear any of what Haakon was still muttering, more to himself than to her.

He fell silent. In the stillness of the clear evening that filtered through the glass of the veranda, the sound of needle on fabric filled the whole room. Once more Haakon spoke:

"Will Miss Felice be coming this week?" It was a question that must have arisen from some private train of thought. Mrs D. looked up from her complicated darning in surprise, distracted from her own reflections.

"Is Felice coming? Yes, tomorrow we're going to prune the hedge behind the new azalea. It's something we should have done earlier, but . . ."

"Last year, I remember, you and I did that job," Haakon interrupted. After a pause he added "If you're agreeable, we could save her the trouble of coming all the way up here for such a trifling matter. It didn't even take us a day last year."

"I think Felice enjoys it. She is becoming fond of the garden. In less than a year she has got to know it as well as I do." Then, sounding like somebody about to disclose a much-pondered secret, she added: "Do you know what I like about her? Her ability to look without envy on the good things other people own, and to grow fond of them without being possessive."

"This garden of yours," Haakon asked ironically, "this garden which arouses emotions, affection, possessiveness . . . couldn't it . . . couldn't it all just be a figment of your imagination?" Mrs D. paid no attention; her thoughts were still fully occupied with Felice.

"A rare ability, my dear," she said. "Few have it. Like being able to put the concept of freedom into practice." Her words froze Haakon's vague gesture of derision in mid-air, but, being well-mannered by nature, she did not exploit her advantage, simply lowering her gaze once more to the white cloth, stretched and tormented by her clumsy stitches, and carefully inserting the white cotton thread.

Haakon watched the glint of the needle in silence for a while, and he sensed that his face, as a wax mask, was stamped with the pout of a sulky child, his bottom lip protruding slightly – a boyhood habit which always re-surfaced when he dropped his guard, safe in the knowledge that no one was watching.

*   *   *

The next day the drawing-room clock had not struck nine when Felice, exercising her tenant's right of way, looked in at the veranda doors and, stopping on the threshold, pronounced a forthright, imperative, "May I come in?"

"Yes of course Felice," Mrs D. said, "do come in and have a cup of coffee with us. Then we'll start work right away." Haakon rose too, with awkward gallantry, but did not approach her — he remained where he was, tongue-tied.

Felice sat down at the table. Her manners were perfect but quite natural, and she was reserved; she would never have made an unnecessary gesture or betrayed the slightest unease. There was nothing studied or artificial in all this. Sitting opposite her, Haakon avoided meeting her eye, leaving the two women to slip once more into the intimacy to which even he was now becoming accustomed. Excluded from a conversation that did not concern him, he swallowed the last of his coffee rather hurriedly and stood up, noisily scraping his chair back from the table. To his mother, who had looked up at him in surprise, he announced he would be out all day; he planned to climb the mountain above Bergen, without any particular destination in mind, for as long as the fancy took him. It was a beautiful day and she should not expect him back for lunch.

"I do envy you," Felice said with a smile, and their eyes met for a long glance. Mrs D., leaning over the sink to wash the cups, made no gesture or comment. Soon after came the sound of the yard door closing and Haakon's rapid footsteps on the flagstones.

"I'm ready now Felice, we can start," said Mrs D. As she led the way out into the garden she seemed troubled by a slight, barely perceptible anxiety.

THIRTEEN

FELICE'S ENVY KEPT him company throughout his long walk on Bergen mountain. So aware was Haakon of her presence that he rediscovered a childhood habit of his: that of holding detailed imaginary conversations with a non-existent companion. In this way he talked to her for a long while, even embarking on a complex discussion, divided into sections and geometrically precise. Questions and answers interwove in perfect alternation with meaningful silences, emphasising the subtle pleasure of a complete understanding between two people. Haakon had never had friends intimate enough to talk to freely. Of freedom, moreover, he had his own – disciplined – concept. It did not mean the chaos of unrestrained ideas and the Babel of competing voices, but rather their methodical arrangement into a composition. Speech would not flow any the less naturally for being ordered; on the contrary it would give rise to a deeper emotional understanding and the knowledge of the real nature of his being, which he knew to be silent, aloof, waiting for the propitious moment.

The tissue of everyday conversation, beginning with the few words he exchanged with his mother, left him feeling painfully awkward and forced him to compress his thoughts to the point of unintelligibility.

Talking to Felice was easy. In the course of a walk he went on every year, so that he knew even the stones by heart and the same perceptions, the same sensations cropped up along the way; on that walk he passed from one subject to another effortlessly, his mind even contemplating bold sorties into shadowy zones that he would never have explored in a real conversation. And his thoughts divided nimbly and lucidly into two strands in order to lend both ideas and a voice to Felice.

She was thirty. From the vantage-point of his own years Haakon treated her with kindly attention and, at times, surprise, dispensing blandishments and reproof where her certainties had not yet been tempered by experience. He was also surprised at himself: not so much for the wisdom of his discourse, but for its ease.

He walked on along the deserted path which led away from Bergen and disappeared into the distance – a grassless furrow through the sparse mountain vegetation. He never brought anything with him on these expeditions, for, as long as he was walking, he feared neither hunger nor thirst. So he made good progress, his only concern being to take care, out of a residue of decorum (and even though the path was empty as far as the eye could see), not to murmur questions and answers under his breath, or speak them out loud when he warmed to his subject.

He had no specific destination and was free at any time to turn back or stray off the track. It was in the middle of one of his satisfying conversations with Felice (he was telling her about his love for solitude), that, in an abrupt summons back to reality, it occurred to him that he had only to return home for Felice herself to take her place in the conversation, with arguments of her own, in her own real voice, with the inflections Haakon was now attributing to her as he painstakingly recreated even the subtlest nuances of her speech in his industrious memory. If he had gone back, the chessboard of their conversation would have had two players to move the pieces: white for Felice and black for Haakon. But it was not yet time to relinquish the advantages of solitude, which allowed him to procrastinate, to forget even the merest possibility of dissonance. And so the dialogue continued, harmonious, regular, one move at a time and no abrupt changes of direction.

At this very moment perhaps, Felice was talking to his mother about flowers. They would be pruning the hedge with masculine vigour, neither of them troubled by the heat, even at the height of a sun-drenched day – and all the while the young woman would be thinking of the cool air on the mountain above Bergen, below which there fanned out a panorama of the fjord.

Haakon walked on. Beyond a hump in the path he glimpsed the shape of a house which he knew to be only an optical illusion, a play of the light on a pile of stones; he would reach there and possibly go further on, to a pond too small to merit the name of lake. He would plunge his feet in the mountain water and rest, no longer thinking of anything. Up there they would not even talk any more.

He strode on, but not before he had asked under his breath, "Are you tired, Felice?"

Her reply was a silent negative: just a resolute shake of the head.

FOURTEEN

AS HAAKON SET FOOT in the house he was brimming with a novel emotion. He delighted in the secrecy of it, even though there was something in his movements – a new-found agility in his shoulders, a suppleness about his neck as he freed it with one swift tug at his sweater – something which gave away a fraction of his secret.

He had expected to find his mother in the kitchen, but discovered her instead sitting in the armchair on the veranda, her feet up on a stool, smoking, her eyes half-closed. Observing her thus, one would have said that the world, the very house around her had no weight or substance; not even in sleep does one surrender so completely, Haakon thought. He decided it would be best to retrace his steps, go up to his room and reappear later, when his mother had become her usual self again.

As it was, she called out: "You're not disturbing me in the least, Haakon," though without changing position: her only movement was to lift the cigarette to her lips then let her arm fall slowly back beside her body.

"I thought you were asleep," explained Haakon, already feeling awkward. He remained standing by her side without looking at her, uncertain whether to go to his room as he had intended, or to sit down with her on the veranda.

"I will just finish my cigarette, dear, then I'll get busy right away." Nothing in her tone promised the slightest action, the slightest gesture. She looked completely happy, sitting there. That "dear" addressed to her son sounded odd now too, and Haakon found it hard to identify with it. And yet she was not being insincere. The garden lay spread out before them, shining in the evening light: the tidied lawn, the evenly pruned hedge which now looked more rigid and austere than ever.

"Why don't you sit down for a minute?" Mrs D. suggested, indicating a small armchair on her left. "You must be tired."

Haakon did not reply. His eyes were fixed on the shadow of the house which was lengthening across the lawn.

"Dinner won't be ready for another half an hour, will it?" he asked, then hastily corrected himself. "No, sorry, I didn't express myself properly, sorry – I don't want to disturb you; there's no hurry. I was just thinking that in the meantime I could go for a dip. There isn't a breath of wind and the water will be warm after all the sun we've had today."

Mrs D. had never considered the lake as anything but an aesthetic feature to be admired from the veranda or – when it was raining or the snow smothered its shores – from a window; at any event always at a distance, like a fragile ornament. Her husband, on the

64

other hand, had been in the habit of going for swims, after which he would return to the house looking like a silvery Neptune, heavy with the weight of his last years. Her feelings for him hovered somewhere between pity for such manifest old age and contempt for his dishevelled state, which emphasised the extent of his fatigue. At such times she would mask her antipathy with the solicitous gesture of draping a robe over his shoulders and hurrying him to get dressed so as not to catch cold.

She looked up at Haakon and noticed a furrow running down the middle of his forehead.

"I should have thought a whole day in the mountains would have worn you out. A dip in the bath upstairs might be more like it." Her tone was unintentionally ironic, but Haakon did not notice.

"It's been a wonderful day," he said, mainly to himself, smiling with unutterable pleasure. "I've never felt better and the lake should be warm at this time of day – the sun hasn't gone down." He was still standing at his mother's side and could not quite make up his mind to move.

"And tomorrow?" he suddenly asked. "Tomorrow will you and . . . will you be gardening again?"

"Of course. Days like these shouldn't be wasted – and in the afternoon I have a few things to see to in town." She extinguished her cigarette and rose to go into the kitchen. Haakon darted ahead of her and practically ran up the stairs. Soon afterwards Mrs D. heard him come down; then, in the almost complete silence, the lapping of the water down at the shore turned to a convulsive splashing, which settled into the rhythm of a swimmer's strokes.

Over dinner they barely spoke to each other, but both insinuated, into what little conversation there was, the memory of some secret pleasure their day had given them. They piled subject upon subject, made vague allusions, disregarding one another, each their own witness, at odds with the other's recollections. Both eventually fell silent from embarrassment, or perhaps from a stubborn reserve. Haakon yielded first, allowing his mother the privilege of being the centre of his attention which was becoming more and more sincere by the minute. She was talking about Felice.

"I must say, she is exceptionally strong – and so agile. To prune the hedge we had to use a ladder and I was not at all sure she would be steady on it, or that reaching out with the shears in her hand might not be a bit . . . well, risky." She paused to nibble at a piece of bread while, with her fork, she broke the herrings up into small pieces on her plate. "One of her good qualities is never to belittle other people's anxieties. She assured me that she would take care not to do anything dangerous, and she can be taken at her word. She climbed up confidently, though I preferred not to let go of the foot of the ladder, in case she lost her balance – but she would have managed perfectly well on her own."

"She would make a good mountain-climber," Haakon commented with a half-smile.

"I don't think climbing would interest her much."

"I thought she herself said this morning that . . ."

66

"She has the exceptionally good manners to show an interest in everything that is said to her," Mrs D. remarked, stealing a furtive glance at her son sitting opposite her. Then she turned her gaze away, towards what she could see of their masterpiece, the hedge, and gave a smile of satisfaction.

Haakon got up from the table, pushing his chair back with an unpleasant scraping sound; he did not apologise.

"There's some cake left over from our lunch. Would you like a slice?" his mother called after him as he went out, but no reply came from the veranda. Perhaps Haakon had not heard her, perhaps she had not caught his answer. In any case she cut herself a piece – just a sliver, from pure greed – and put the plate away.

Haakon stood on the veranda, a strange tingling sensation in his hands and arms. He toyed with his cigarette before lighting it, tapping it on the handrail of the portico, then struck a match. Darkness was rising from the lake slowly, but already the burning cigarette was a vibrant point in the night.

FIFTEEN

IT WAS RAINING. He became aware of it in the moment between sleeping and waking, from the distinctive echo of sounds outside the window and the muffled patter of raindrops on the grass. He thought of his mother, who would not be able to work in the garden, and of Felice, who would not be travelling up from Bergen, from her father's greenhouses, to tend the hedges and flowers around their house. He went down to breakfast earlier than usual without shaving or making any effort over his appearance, despite his mother's disapproval. Mrs D. could not bear slovenliness first thing in the morning. It caused her intense annoyance – an annoyance never expressed in a single comment, only in a mute, resentful glance.

Felice was sitting at the kitchen table, stirring a bowlful of something which Haakon could not quite make out. He saw her raise her head to utter a few words of laconic greeting, with the air of one who must not be disturbed. He regretted his dishevelled appearance and smoothed his hair down with his hand, embarrassed by his wholly unexpected proximity to the girl, though she gave no sign of having noticed anything. She was distracted from her task by Haakon's clumsy clattering of plates and asked if there was anything she could do to help.

"Absolutely not. In Hamburg I manage very well on my own," he replied, forgetting even to thank her. He seemed offended, as if Felice had criticised him.

"You can sit down to table in the dining-room, Haakon, I'll make the coffee." His mother's voice, issuing from behind Felice's back, conclusively disposed of Haakon's embarrassment by officially excluding him from the world of the two women. A few minutes later, alone with a newspaper which did not interest him, he ate his breakfast and pondered his mother's words to Felice: "I'll be with you in a minute. I'm just going to get things ready in the other room. Haakon hates having breakfast in public." They must both have smiled. So he ate alone, looking out at the garden, which was dark green from the pouring rain, feeling disconcerted and ill at ease. Less than a fortnight remained before his return to Hamburg.

Since it rained all morning he yielded to idleness, not finding, and indeed not seeking, any more profitable occupation than sitting out on the veranda contemplating the grey lake. The chatter from the kitchen kept him company for a while, then he forgot all about it, until he was suddenly struck by the silence, more deafening than an explosion. It was past midday; the house seemed deserted. He crept like a thief into the empty kitchen, then into the dining-room, where the remains of his breakfast had been cleared away. He was struck as though for the first time by the neatness of the rooms, the silence, the way nothing was out of place and the house was so orderly – almost as if it were about to be vacated rather than lived in from day to day.

"You were looking for me, Haakon?" Mrs D. was standing in the veranda doorway behind him, her raincoat dripping wet, a scarf over her hair, her eyelashes glittering with raindrops.

The image Mrs D. presented to her son grew stranger every day, unfamiliar to him, and elusive. His mother was a woman of few affections: the one thing she loved, tenaciously and above all else, was a world of her own creation, around which she made everything revolve. Of course her new-found solidarity with Felice sprang from this world, from her garden, and Haakon watched from the sidelines in the role he was destined to, because he had never been part of this Eden his mother had created and tended.

"Lunch will be ready soon," said Mrs D. from the corridor where she was hanging up her raincoat. With characteristic efficiency she had everything arranged to perfection in a quarter of an hour and had prepared a lunch that Haakon ate without appetite.

"I don't suppose you have been able to do any gardening today," he enquired in a roundabout way, so as not to seem curious. And she, untroubled, with the patience of one who has all the time in the world, replied calmly:

"It can wait until tomorrow, if the weather improves, or even the day after." She gave no hint of where or how she had spent her morning.

"So . . . so Miss Felice has gone back to Bergen?"

"No, she is going to be in the keeper's cottage all afternoon, sorting out her things."

"Ah," Haakon let slip under his breath, but not loudly enough to be heard. He retired behind the newspaper he had been reading earlier.

Felice was still putting the table linen in a drawer when she heard a discreet knock on the window-pane. She looked up, placed an ironed table-cloth on the chest of drawers, and went to the door to greet her visitor.

"I've come at a bad time, haven't I?"

"Not at all, it's perfectly alright. Come in." And she stood aside to make way for Haakon.

SIXTEEN

FELICE MANAGED TO make tea with the few things she had to hand in her still disordered house. They drank it unceremoniously at the table, on an ill-fitting cloth which the girl had been about to iron and put away in a drawer, but now spread over part of the table-top (it was not large enough to cover the whole). The cups did not match and the milk was left to gleam white in the bottle, Felice having neglected to seek out a nobler vessel.

"I haven't been inside this house for years." Haakon was gazing around the room with a half-smile. Felice made no reply but drank her tea calmly, looking up at him only when he continued, in an awkward, hesitant voice: "It feels so strange that it should be let out now!" His second smile of embarrassment met with the same reception as the first.

"I imagine you want to know why I thought of asking your mother for this house." This last remark of Felice's was not a question so much as the articulation of a thought Haakon himself was unable to voice. Her tone was stern, yet there was nothing offensive or arrogant in her outspokenness. Haakon felt relieved.

"It is certainly true that my mother has not

mentioned anything about the matter – why you came to live here, I mean."

"I shouldn't think she would have wished to say anything. Your mother is a discreet woman. When I spoke to her she didn't ask any questions, merely assessed the possible benefits of the idea, and rightly so. And as the benefits were mutual, we drew up an agreement."

"So you will be staying here for a few years, I imagine? That would be a good thing, really, because – and please forgive my interfering in a matter which has nothing to do with me – I am assessing the situation too, from my own point of view. I am not involved in your agreement in any way, naturally enough . . ." Felice was totally impassive, but listened attentively and looked Haakon straight in the eye so that his words stuck in his throat for a moment. "My assessment is very personal, but I am sure you will understand. I'm thinking about my mother's age and my work in Hamburg, which I would prefer not to give up before I have to. Hamburg is a long way away. Perhaps your being here could be a . . . how can I put it without your misunderstanding me? . . . a source of security, a real help."

While he was speaking Felice stood up to put her cup in the sink, leaving on the table the small saucepan holding the rest of the tea. She moved unhurriedly, left the tap running for a while, shifted the cup to make sure it did not slip, then finally turned to Haakon:

"I will be like any other next-door neighbour." She

73

spoke the words distinctly, as if to impress them indelibly on his mind.

"I'm sorry if I may have seemed indiscreet. I thought I had noticed a friendly rapport between you and my mother, a closeness . . ."

She interrupted at once:

"I know about plants professionally, Mr Haakon, and your mother loves them."

The subject was closed, and Haakon grew confused, losing the thread of any possible conversation in the face of such a solid wall of reserve. He still had a little tea in the bottom of his cup and, gripped by a childhood inhibition, the maternal decree that in other people's houses he should never leave anything unfinished, he drank it to the last drop, filling his mouth and swallowing it at one gulp.

Viewed thus, from the inside, the cottage seemed dingy, dug as it was into the hillside, with no view of the lake – that sweep of water which was the greatest charm of the main house.

"But if I am not mistaken, you wanted to know how I came to live here, and why." Now Felice was pressing him on the very questions he no longer had the courage to ask.

Haakon put down his empty cup, which was slightly chipped – he had run his tongue over the rim to feel its unevenness. He pushed it away from him towards the centre of the table and slowly rose to his feet, his movements encumbered by who knows what burden.

"I think I have taken far too much of your time already. You had other things to do; I'm sorry. It comes of not having any work commitments — I'm speaking personally of course — I forget that other people do. Please excuse my lack of consideration." He turned and faced the door into the yard. Whatever effect he may have been expecting from his words, they appeared to have fallen on deaf ears. Felice did not ask him to stay, not even out of perfunctory politeness; nor did she return to the unanswered question. She let him go to the door.

"Good afternoon, Mr Haakon." And that was all, accompanied this time by just the hint of a smile.

As he climbed the steps in the steep path which emerged at a bend in the main drive he noticed that some of the stone slabs, previously dislodged, were back in place, and firmly set into the ground, while the surrounding grass had been cut back neatly. Felice's hand was apparent in every detail of this neatness. Haakon reflected that, little by little, the whole cottage would be re-fashioned by this same methodical mind.

His mother's black house appeared before him through a vista he had never once noticed in all those years; he wondered if a tree or two had been cut down, or at least pruned, to form a gap that would link the two houses. Haakon couldn't say, and regretted that his taking the place for granted should have led him to overlook something so important.

Mrs D. was not in the house when Haakon peered through the drawing-room door, nor could he see her in the garden. From the silence it seemed that not a living soul had passed by there for some time. He climbed the stairs, stole into his bedroom, his heart

75

racing with the fear of discovery and, from the window, surveyed the garden down towards the lake. There his mother was, by the shore, going over the grass with a light rake, as thoroughly as if she were cleaning the drawing-room carpet.

Years before, when Haakon had assumed he would stay in Bergen, and the idea of working abroad had not even arisen, he had tried to persuade his mother that a dog would appreciate all the space in the garden, and would be company. He could not even remember now what explanation she had given for the curt refusal which had crushed the suggestion at birth. Possibly none at all, just that incontestable "no". In those days it was natural that Mrs D. should not even consider sharing her Earthly Paradise with any living creature outside the plant kingdom. But now behold: into Paradise had come Felice, who occupied a modest but permanent space and would, in time, come to occupy a larger and larger one.

The sturdy figure of the old lady was moving in silhouette down by the water's edge, as she swiftly thrust the rake forward and dragged it back towards her.

Haakon opened the window and, with thumb and forefinger, quickly and furtively flicked his cigarette-end out on to the lawn. The butt completed a small parabola and landed on the grass, not far from the veranda steps.

It was almost time for dinner.

SEVENTEEN

TWO PACES FORWARD, one back, and the rhythm of the rake gathering up the leaves strewn over the lawn, along with what recently cut grass had escaped the drum of the lawn-mower. Mother and son were moving along together: she absorbed in her task, he at her side, hands in pockets, keeping her company. Purely from courtesy he might occasionally bend down to place an unruly blade of grass back on the pile. The midday sun was gentle and pleasant on Haakon's bare arms, tanned from his walks in the Bergen mountains.

"Only one week's holiday left, Haakon," Mrs D. remarked, but there was no particular feeling or emotion in her voice — it was merely an accurate statement of fact.

"She will be an excellent neighbour for you. I'm referring to Miss Felice, of course," Haakon leant down to return an errant leaf back to the pile.

"Thank you Haakon, there's no need to do that. Don't bend down: I've got to go over the whole lawn again in any case. You were talking about Felice. Yes, she will be. The quality I value above all others is intelligence; she is someone I will be able to rely on; she is also courageous and has her own personal concept of freedom, if you see what I mean. I've sometimes wondered how many other girls would have actually gone through with what seemed at first like a mere flight of fancy – deciding to move up here, out of town, when in Bergen she had everything, except . . ."

"So her father will be left on his own."

"My dear Haakon, that is the natural law of compensation. In this world there is a constant amount of solitude, and if my own has to some extent come to an end, another must come into being to restore the balance." She wielded the rake with vigour – two paces forward, one back – and every now and then set aside a small, neat mound of leaves and grass.

"And when Felice gets married . . ."

"Felice, naturally, will not marry." She gently tapped the rake to free a lump of earth from its teeth.

"I wouldn't have thought thirty was so conclusive an age, even for a woman," Haakon objected, taking care to sound casual, as if merely making conversation. He received no reply. The lake glowed brighter than ever in the sunlight and mirrored the deep green of the surrounding mountains. He had a sudden vision of the watery reflection he saw every day from the window of his Hamburg flat: the white buildings plunged in the still lake.

"How can you be so sure that Miss Felice will not marry? I confess it has occurred to me that the keeper's lodge would be just the place to meet a fiancé her family disapproved of."

Mrs D.'s expression took on a sudden frostiness, but

instantly melted into a smile in which all ill-feeling had abated.

"You too! Your father would have been exactly the same. People like you never realise that instinct has its own rationality and is sustained by a hundred deep motives. Those are precisely the depths you fail to penetrate." She was still smiling, perhaps even mocking him with her graciously superior manner. "You shouldn't blame yourself, Haakon, believe me. It's only a question of being sensitive; some things are perfectly obvious if one applies a minimum of sensitivity. But that was never a strong point in your father's family, any member of it, and you are quite clearly one of them!"

They did not return to the subject. Haakon soon stopped keeping pace with his mother's to-ing and fro-ing, and sat down on a part of the lawn that had already been cleared, facing the lake.

The cleaning of the lawn continued, with what Haakon considered to be insane regularity, for another two hours. He counted twenty-two strokes of the rake in the section between the stone seat and the top of the drive – and Mrs D. covered this same area fully three times over.

Even as a child Haakon had been obsessed with numbers. He would seek out all their possible combinations and interpret them as messages – auspicious or otherwise – from Fate. One Christmas he was given a skipping rope with dark blue wooden handles and, as soon as the days started turning warm, he took to retiring to the yard behind the house, where he would skip and count how far he could get without tripping. Above all it was essential not to trip between 100 and 111, 200 and 222 and so on – each time from the round hundred to the point where the three digits were identical. He would concentrate like a mountaineer on a difficult traverse, feeling his arms tense up with the effort and the swift rhythm of his feet quicken further with the strain of surviving the danger zone. The tension dropped once he was safely outside that bewitched territory.

His mother completed twenty-two pulls of the rake between the seat to the drive: her full quota. He rose and re-joined her as she folded back the mouth of a large jute sack in readiness for the dry leaves.

"Isn't it strange that Felice is not here to help you?" he said, and smiled with a touch of mockery which was not lost on his mother. She let it pass, bending over to press the leaves down into the bottom of the sack, then raised her face, beaded with sweat. Peering round Haakon, she looked up to the top of the path. Felice was walking down towards the lake.

EIGHTEEN

IT WAS HAAKON'S HABIT, on the first day of his last week, to go to Bergen station and reserve a seat on the train to Oslo. Every year he asked for assurances that it would be leaving on schedule, because a five-minute delay was enough to risk his missing the ferry to Travemünde. From there he was certain, if not of punctuality, at least of the ship connecting with the Hamburg express. With the ticket, bought and paid for, in his pocket, he would return home, and thus an initial severing of ties with his mother, with the world of the lake, the garden, and the quiet order of the rooms, was made official. Over the following days both he and Mrs D. would mark the passing of the hours by imagining, in detail, the events and circumstances of the coming journey.

"By this time five days from now," she would say, "you will already be on board the ferry;" or "In three days time your train will be just about to enter the outskirts of Oslo." They did this from melancholy, or perhaps the need to accustom themselves to the idea of departure and solitude.

This year Mrs D. was ready, as ever, for their rites of departure. It was the morning of Monday the 7th of July, and Haakon was required to catch the tram to the station, go through the usual ceremony and be back before noon. This particular Monday the 7th of July it was raining and Haakon overslept, so that he did not hear, or pretended not to hear, his mother tapping on the door.

When he awoke fully, unconcerned that it was too late for his usual errand, he clasped his hands behind his head and yielded himself up to inertia, devoid of willpower. His thoughts drifted effortlessly from his body to pursue another Haakon as, faithful to the yearly ritual, this imaginary twin busied himself rummaging for a jersey in his drawer, put on his galoshes and the mackintosh he only wore on his Bergen holidays and, rigged out like a sailor in a comic opera, strode briskly out to the tram stop. His mind could have counted the steps of this other Haakon, spelled out his words and seen, even felt, the money for the ticket and reservation. Too late to go for a stroll through the town: the midday tram had already opened its doors to the passengers.

In reality, however, this time everything was taking place within the modest confines of a bed, between barely disturbed sheets, warmed by a drowsy body. The ten o'clock tram had already passed the gate, indeed by now would almost certainly be stopped under the station portico, next to the entrance to the booking hall, and it was as if its trip had been made in vain.

But now the journey and its propitiatory rites were fading into the blurred horizons of his mind, from which, with confident stride, advanced Felice. Only the day before when, from the look in his mother's eyes, he had guessed at the girl's presence, he had once more resolved to study her face and movements closely. She was not a beautiful woman, not even blessed with any charming imperfections, any of those dissonances which are more captivating than flawless beauty. Her step was certainly assured, however, and confidently seconded by the energetic swing of her arms. She would have been a good companion on excursions for, to look at, the whole of her body seemed attuned to the idea of physical exertion, but was dominant, not subordinate to it.

Haakon raised his head slightly to clasp his hands more comfortably behind the nape of his neck, then sank back on to the pillow; but neither of his day-dreams – his trip into town or Felice's steady stride – came back to him. His father used to walk in that way and, with the aloofness of the born solitary, he would wear out the few companions who joined him, albeit seldom, on his long mountain expeditions. But he, old Mr D., would never have dreamt of devoting his energies to an artifice: "Your garden, Agnes my dear, is an act of forgery. Yours more than others because it is more beautiful," he would say in a tone of irony and indulgent mockery, considering himself above such a limiting passion. "Gardens are for those who are afraid of space," he told her and, as good as his word, never lifted a finger to come to the aid of a plant, nor offered to help his wife, not even when he saw her lean out from the top rung of the ladder to clip a tall hedge.

During the month of her husband's illness, Mrs D. had divided her time impartially between his bedroom and the plants and flowers in her garden, never failing in her duties to either. In the sickroom, alone at her husband's side, she waited resolutely for the end to come. Haakon could still clearly remember how her lips were less tense and her touch light at last when, on the morning after the funeral, she had gone down to remove the straw from around her two azaleas. Mr D. had died in May, when even the most delicate young plants can be exposed to the open air without shelter.

He would get the ticket tomorrow. So, with his mind unburdened and the day ahead a great expanse of time to be divided up as he pleased, Haakon slowly unwound himself from the sheets, slid out of bed and got dressed as if he had all the time in the world. He looked out at the rain falling on the garden and felt glad that the thick clouds promised no respite. On the back of a used sheet of paper he left a note for his mother, telling her not to expect him back for lunch or even for dinner, and to leave the key under the cushion of the deck chair on the veranda. This long-standing arrangement dated back to his adolescence and allowed Mrs D. to feel she had not lost all her authority. He tiptoed noiselessly down the stairs and left the note in full view on the hall table, next to the telephone. He found his mackintosh on the coat rack in the back porch, put it on, then went out by the door at the end of the corridor, into the yard where he used to go skipping as a child. From there an over-grown path of steep granite steps offered a far shorter route than the main drive, reaching the front gates in a matter of yards. Nobody used it any more; Haakon himself had practically forgotten about it. The steps and the grass were glistening, and after he had gone a few paces down the path Haakon's coat was also gleaming wet.

NINETEEN

''HE WILL BE LEAVING on Sunday, by the ten o'clock train, I presume. I might even say I'm positive. If nothing else, Haakon is a creature of habit – I always know what he'll be doing, and how and when he'll be doing it. The slightest variation upsets him. That can be a positive quality when dealing with others – I'm not saying it's a failing. What I've always thought he does lack, though, is imagination. When I was pregnant and I could sense it was going to be a boy (I desperately wanted my first child to be a boy – the sex of the others didn't matter. I never dreamt there would only ever be the one . . . but that's another story) – as I was saying, when I was still expecting him I had already chosen a name: Haraald. Do you know the story, Felice, of the first King of Norway, Haraald the Fair? The one who swore to his betrothed that he would never comb his hair, or cut it, till he had united all the Lands of the North under one sceptre? You don't? I had read the sagas as a girl; I knew them by heart and found them more entertaining than romantic novels. Those tales of the kings of old had an awe-inspiring quality to them. So my son had to be Haraald. My husband also had his own ideas about names, and we argued the question at length; we enjoyed our discussions, but we got quite heated. Names, Felice, are precise indications of character. My husband insisted on our son being called Haakon because he had a mystical theory about the power of the name. You see, he too was following a historical thread, a memory: an archbishop of Stavanger, I don't know exactly when, but at the time of the last Vikings. So I gave up insisting on my long-haired king. As it turned out, we were both wrong." She smiled sarcastically.

Mrs D. and Felice were sitting in the dining-room, looking out at the uniform grey of the rain. In Bergen, at the height of summer, one occasionally gets long days of unbroken rain. At such times Mrs D., unable to work outside, resigned herself to contemplating her garden through the half-open dining-room windows.

"You could not possibly understand what a disappointment a son is. You, my dear Felice, will never have sons; you will stick to your own path in life; it will be yours alone and will not become entangled in other people's lives. That is for the best. But now let me contradict myself." She gazed intensely at the girl beside her and received a forthright look in reply. "You should have been my daughter," she said, reaching over to clasp Felice's wrist. The young woman did not start or tremble. Seeing that she had drawn no response, Mrs D. grew uneasy and, regretting the gesture, withdrew her hand and lowered her eyes:

"I'm talking too much, my dear; I'm taking too much for granted. And with you, of all people; you who so obviously value reserve and moderation." With each word, there grew in Mrs D.'s voice an implicit request for some sign of solidarity, as when one has made a serious confession.

"How can you be sure I wouldn't have disappointed you as much as, or even more than your son has?" This was not exactly the rush of sympathy she had been hoping for, but it offered a thread which she must not lose hold of. The deepest understandings between two people are born of unlikely conditions, even intolerance. One of the two carves a passage through rock towards the other, every splinter costing a thousand years of patience. Time is a great persuader, Mrs D. thought to herself – normal everyday time, like the hours they shared working in their garden.

"Haakon will be leaving on Sunday," she repeated out loud, and seemed to be on the point of returning to her previous subject, the name of the barbarian king. Instead she got up nimbly from the armchair, looked at her watch and recovered the commanding tone which suited her best: "You had better be getting home now, Felice. Haakon could be back soon – I don't think he really will stay out late tonight – and I'd like to have some dinner ready for him." Her voice was cheerful.

Felice stood up, straightened her skirt out of natural tidiness, not vanity, and pushed the chair back under the table:

"Tomorrow, Madam, I will be at my father's nursery all morning and part of the afternoon. You won't be needing me here: it's bound to rain again tomorrow."

"Of course, Felice. If you would like to join me for

a cup of tea when you get back in the evening, it would be a pleasure to see you."

Felice thanked her without making any promises, and Mrs D. seemed content to leave it at that. Had it not just occurred to her that time was on her side? So she started to savour it little by little, parcelling it out into the minute and thrifty gobbets of one unwilling to squander capital all at once.

Once alone in the house she did not even consider cooking, either for herself or for Haakon: the more feverish her expectation of some event, the less she felt like acting. Motionless as an animal lying in wait, apprehensive at every movement, she sharpened her senses to every least sign or unexpected signal both around or within her. By ten o'clock of an evening silent except for the drumming of the rain on the wood of the veranda, Haakon had still not returned. Mrs D. was fidgeting with the sheet of paper she had found next to the telephone that morning, but finally resigned herself to putting the keys under the cushions on the veranda chair. She closed the dining-room windows tightly, locked the door with two turns of the key and straightened the chairs, even though they were barely out of line. Then, after one final approving glance at the kitchen, she turned off the lights and went upstairs.

TWENTY

HIS LIGHT TREAD on the steps did not disturb the silence of the house. With the hand of a thief, he felt in the dark between the cushions on the veranda chair until his fingers encountered the cold metal key. He found the keyhole by touch, but his eyes had meanwhile become accustomed to the dark, so that he had no need to switch the lights on even in the house. He closed the door carefully, keeping a gentle hand on it, even lifting it slightly so that no creak should pierce the stillness of the night. He instantly recovered the sense of space which he had known as a child when he had played at being blind: fifteen long paces to the bottom of the stairs, twelve steps up the first flight to the landing, then another twelve to the bedroom corridor. His feet found their childhood rhythm, the long strides now short steps – another fifteen of them. His only difficulty lay in suppressing the urge to race up the stairs two at a time.

Once in his room, he calmly prepared himself for insomnia. He feared it less and less; indeed he was now so undaunted by the prospect of a sleepless night that he looked upon it as a gift from the hand of time, liberally dispensed and free of charge. He undressed, draped his wet clothes on a chair, passed a hand through his damp hair, then over his neck and shoulders and stood lost in thought for a moment before putting on his pyjamas.

Finally he got into bed and arranged his light covers in readiness for the sleep that would never come. All the same he went through the motions of his night-time ritual, closing his eyes and curling up as tightly as possible with his hands between his knees. But he did not relax: he could feel his jaw clamped tight and his muscles struggling to dominate his body. So, instead of sleep, there advanced towards him faces and visions, lightly dancing, barely veiled by his eyelids . . . that night when his father had desecrated the roses, like a capricious god, heedless of human affairs, and his mother had been so alone in the face of such an outrage! Now Felice would be there at her side, in a silence that comprehends and remembers all things. Felice was the pure virgin of the garden which Haakon could not enter.

Haakon's days were numbered: five more, then the gates would close behind him and that long arm of sea, the Oslo fjord, would seal his physical separation from the house. He might quite easily never come back. Certain signs told him he never should. In his mind he painted a picture of the house, in summer, without him – his mother able to order her freedom as she chose, down to the very last detail. Felice was part of that freedom: the two dwellings, so very close together, seemed to merge into one house, dominating the lake and the garden.

He threw off his covers and went to the window.

Out there were the black hill, the leaden lake and the darkness of a sky heavy with rain. The weather would stay like this until the morning of his departure; nobody would be able to tend the garden, not even Felice. He sat down in the armchair under the window without noticing the chill of the floor against his bare feet. Very gradually his body was freeing itself from the grip of his muscles; his hands were slipping, releasing the chair-arms; the knots in his limbs were loosening, unravelling.

His thoughts turned to the arrangements for his forthcoming journey as to a duty left unfinished, and one that not even on the morrow perhaps – perhaps not even on the last day of all – would he feel like bothering about. Before him, dressed in white, the capricious god smiled with benevolent derision.

Lying crookedly, his head thrown back on an arm of the chair, his mouth half-open, Haakon slept.

The following morning the weather was unchanged: the rain continued to beat down on the lawn, now sodden and dark, and on the lake. Even so a hooded figure was making its way along the path to the castaway-seat, a figure wrapped in a cloak that reached to the ground and made it impossible to distinguish the form beneath. It was proceeding slowly and ponderously, perhaps hiding or sheltering something under the oilskin. Haakon observed from his bedroom window. An obstinate determination to act, even against all reason, is peculiar to certain characters and intensifies dangerously with age. Yet now, in his mother's stubborn defiance of reason and common sense, Haakon thought he could detect a kind of superiority. Even the most trivial action has two sides to it, one healthy, one unhealthy. Mrs D., tending to her garden in the driving rain, must have been motivated by a higher freedom, by the certainty which comes when heart and mind finally blossom into a deep attachment.

He went downstairs to the drawing-room window; from there the cloaked figure was no longer visible, obscured by the slope down to the lake. Haakon positioned himself close to the window, waiting for it to reappear above the curve of the hill, and sure enough, in a short while, the black cape was moving indistinctly against the green of the grass. Mrs D. was advancing with difficulty, but it was hard to see what was hampering her. All of a sudden she hunched up, bent at the knees, and Haakon thought he caught the convulsive gesture of her hands as they clutched at something under the cloak. Motionless in that position, she finally raised her head in search of help. Haakon stepped away from the window, turned his back to the garden and went into the kitchen where the table was laid for a breakfast that one person had already finished. In total silence, almost holding his breath, he waited for his mother's voice to call out the name of Felice.

TWENTY-ONE

"WOULD YOU MIND very much if we went outside? I find it oppressive in a greenhouse. It's a question of what one's used to, you know." The moment he had entered Haakon had felt the impact of the humid heat trapped beneath the glass roof, to the point that he found it difficult to breathe – his breath was already coming short in any case, as if he had run all the way there and his heartbeat was irregular. He did not at first spot Felice who, they had told him, would definitely be there: she was over at the opposite side of the greenhouse, attending to a potted plant. Haakon reluctantly ventured the short distance to her side, through a damp and pungent zone. He had to pick his way along the narrow passage between the benches, taking care not to brush against the plants set up on long slats resting on brick supports; even the earth beneath them looked moist and permeated with damp heat.

The object of Felice's attentions was a gardenia. The leaves of the young plant were seething with minute creatures which the girl was patiently removing by cleaning leaf after leaf with a rag soaked in some unknown liquid. Absorbed in her task, she made no response to Haakon's request, but continued with the operation as though she had not the slightest intention of altering her plans, particularly for an unexpected visitor.

"Are these plants diseased?" Haakon asked with resigned docility, since the girl was paying him no attention. Meanwhile he watched her swift, light movements. She barely skimmed the surface of each vivid green, fleshy leaf, leaving it free of the unpleasant specks, only to pass on immediately to another – a seemingly endless task.

She replied without taking her hands or eyes off the gardenia:

"Plants may have parasites from time to time, but it is nothing serious, as you see – one just has to deal with them promptly." And at last she looked him directly in the eye, still holding one leaf between her fingers, seeming to stroke it as one might a child's chin.

"Have a look," she invited him. "It has plenty of new leaves and three buds; one of them will be flowering soon. Once it is free of pests it won't suffer any more."

Haakon moved closer to Felice and bent over the plant, examining it with a curiosity which was initially feigned, but soon became almost compulsive. He felt both attracted and repelled, and his eyes dwelt on the very place from which he would most have liked to tear his gaze. Two of the buds were still small, and of a dark green which was barely distinguishable from the deep hue of the leaves, but the colour of the third, the largest and fullest, was diaphanous, blanching. Almost mature enough to open, swollen, it was

95

yielding to the first appearance of the white flower, already discernible through the transparency of the thin green sheath, which was on the point of splitting.

"If the heat makes you so uncomfortable," she finally said, distracting him from his obsessive study of the bud, "we could go out for a moment; I'll come back to this later. You might prefer to talk in my father's office. Follow me, it's over here." She passed the rag swiftly over one last leaf, then put her things away and started down the narrow passage between the benches, leading the way to the door.

In point of fact he had at first planned to write to Felice: either the moment he got back to Hamburg, or even before leaving Bergen, in which case he would have posted the letter at the station. He would have addressed it to the house on the lake – his house. During that solitary morning, as he had wandered the silent rooms while his mother was busy with her tireless ferrying of pots, he had honed and clarified the tone of the letter – without, however, setting pen to paper. His anxieties finally fell into a precise order, and his heart was lightened by the mere thought of action. Then he pictured the white envelope lying in the old letter-box on the railings at the end of the drive, as if the letter were himself, shut out from his own home, waiting for an unknown hand to raise the latch of the little gate, and he decided not to write. It may have been jealousy of that stranger's hand, or a feeling that the stretch of sea between himself and the black house on the lake was growing too deep and impassable – whatever the reason, he did not write. Nor did he even bother about arranging the ticket for Hamburg, though his departure was imminent. Instead he reflected that the glacial woman who had received him in the keeper's lodge might be different in another setting, where talking to her would feel more natural, and he might hear her reply with the ease of that day when he was walking on the mountain.

He changed his clothes and went down to Bergen on foot, a long walk that felt as necessary to him as a mountaineer's acclimatisation. It was just past midday when Haakon walked through the station arcade, hearing the clock strike the hour, and decided that he would take her to lunch down by the port. He crossed the station yard and left on the opposite side, in front of the old hotel. At the nearby newspaper kiosk he asked the way to the nursery, and the man leant over the counter to point out the street that led to the old quarter, at the foot of the mountain. Thus he had finally reached Felice.

TWENTY-TWO

SHE CURTLY REFUSED to lunch with him, then, more conciliatory, explained that she disliked having meals in company.

"I enjoy eating and I like my mealtimes to be restful."

"You've stayed to lunch with my mother though, if I'm not mistaken."

"Yes, of course," she agreed, but did not elaborate. As she spoke she ushered him into her father's office; a small room with an internal window opening into the greenhouse. It seemed to Haakon to be filled with the same close, humid atmosphere they had just left. He found it just as suffocating. Felice, who by contrast seemed quite at ease there, gave him a consoling smile:

"How unlike you are! You and your mother, I mean. How little you have in common . . . except that you seem to share the same ordered, methodical outlook."

"I'll be leaving on the 15th — that's this Sunday — as I have done every year for the past seventeen years. I'm methodical in that too. My mother will have told you that I lack imagination."

Felice raised her eyebrows slightly, hesitated for a moment, then, out of honesty, gave a nod.

"This year," he said, "I've let my imagination run

so wild that I've not even booked my return ticket yet."

"Your mother is certain you've already bought it," she replied, observing him more intently.

"In point of fact I won't go home today without doing what my mother expects of me. The station is quite close. But I must confess . . ." and here he hunched down, staring fixedly at his hands; the protruding veins, the well-cared-for nails, the heavily wrinkled knuckles. "I must confess I would rather not leave." Felice had sat back a little, very upright in her chair; in order, Haakon supposed, to keep a suitable distance. "Does this thought of mine disturb you too, Miss Felice?"

"It's none of my business. You'll be raising the matter with your mother, I imagine, as you see fit of course."

The room was stifling. Haakon loosened the neck of his sweater, aware of Felice in front of him, calm and self-possessed like a queen patiently granting him an audience. He thought his confusion must be making the girl feel a little sorry for him, and rather impatient. He wiped a thin film of sweat from around his mouth.

"I don't think my mother will want me to stay on." He looked Felice straight in the eye, but she was so tranquil, so remote. He was talking to her from such an immense distance that his instinct was to raise his voice. The poky little office no longer seemed large enough to hold both of them, so wide was the gulf between them. "If I'm not mistaken, you are more than just a next-door neighbour; or, if that's indeed

99

all you are, you won't remain so. But I shouldn't want you to reply now," he said, stopping her with a gesture. "It takes time."

Felice took a deep breath, like an athlete gathering strength for one last effort. She placed her hands on the desk-top and splayed her fingers wide. One could see that her body and her mind were equally efficient.

"You are hinting at something you don't wish to state plainly." She smiled indulgently. "You have every right to use whatever words you want. I have become your rival, quite unintentionally, and if you think it necessary we can spell out . . ." Here she gave a conciliatory nod, "we can spell out exactly what makes us rivals." She stopped for a moment and allowed Haakon to sink into his silence, to lose himself in it. "But I am sure we don't need to. People can reach an understanding by the most unlikely routes. You will know better than I how numerous these paths are, how infinite. Why limit yourself to a single one and give it an absolute importance which it doesn't really have? You want to know for certain something which soon you won't even remember."

"How can you tell how long my memory . . . ?"

"You're leaving on Sunday. As soon as the ship is out of sight of Oslo Town Hall . . . You *are* sailing from Oslo, aren't you?" Haakon nodded, disconcerted by this trivial digression, so concrete and immediate. "Once Oslo is behind you, for a whole year all Norway will seem heaven knows how many miles away. Your mind will return to other things. It always has and it always will." She fell silent again and looked at him pensively: "A year, believe me Mr Haakon, is a long long time!"

"Felice!" and this time his voice rose in earnest, to pursue and catch up with this strange sibyl whose oracular response had descended on him, leaving him far behind, with no trail to follow. Confronted with the young woman's composure, he felt utterly disconcerted. She had not lost her poise even on hearing her name almost shouted. She nodded at him to speak — she was listening.

"I leave on Sunday. Would you grant me your company on one of the five days I have left? Come with me to Torpo. It is the village where my mother and father were married. I don't know it myself, I've never seen it. Will you come?"

Felice's was the same soft voice he remembered from their walk on Bergen mountain; her head had the same resolute tilt.

"You have four days left, Mr Haakon," she corrected him with a smile, "and I am afraid I do not have any time to give you. Not now. Perhaps on some other occasion . . ."

"I leave on Sunday!" he repeated, as though obsessed with the idea.

Felice nodded pensively. "You will be back next year, same as ever. Lack of imagination may prove to be a virtue after all." She appeared to be joking, trifling with him. The room had grown small again, the two of them closer together.

"Your mother has also asked me to accompany her to Torpo. She hasn't been back there since her wedding day – fifty years ago, if I'm not mistaken? We are going at the end of the summer."

Haakon slowly rose to his feet and ran a hand through his hair, which kept falling over his eyes – he could see his reflection in the window, against the greenery of the hothouse. He made a vague gesture of farewell, but Felice offered him her hand, saying:

"Have a good trip, Mr Haakon. I don't think we will be meeting again – not in these next few days."

TWENTY-THREE

HIS MOTHER HAD already seen to the taxi, booked for twenty-past nine on Sunday morning. Haakon found out that same Wednesday at dinner, when mother and son met after several days during which their timetables had not coincided. Mrs D. made it clear, nonetheless, that she had never for one moment doubted his loyalty to a custom confirmed by seventeen years of practice: he would be leaving on the usual day, at the usual hour.

"I thought forty minutes should be ample to get everything done. After all, it's only a matter of loading your luggage into the taxi and locking up the house – naturally I will come to see you off. The roads should be quiet at that time on a Sunday. They were last year, remember? Although, now I come to think of it, you didn't have long to wait before the train left; only enough time to buy a paper and find your compartment. Would you like me to ask the taxi to come earlier?"

Haakon shook his head. His gaze wandered from her to the garden, then back again. Of course, he remembered his last departure as if it were yesterday, remembered it down to the last detail: with the toe of his shoe he had flicked aside a ball of paper that had been lying on the platform in front of his compartment door. The journey he would make in three days time, on the other hand, that identical journey with its identical arrangements, was somehow impossible to picture. He thanked her for her thoughtfulness and refused her offer to help him pack.

"I have some experience of suitcases and a system of my own," he reminded her with a smile. "Anyway, I have a few days left. You don't want us to spend the rest of our time talking about nothing else but the journey do you?" He leant towards her, staring into her eyes, questioning her more deeply than he could in words.

Mrs D. drew back in irritation. "My dear Haakon, I am simply trying to ease your departure in any way I can." Her smile returned, and she too looked into the garden. From where she sat, the azalea was just visible through the kitchen door, green and flourishing. "Perhaps this time it will manage to survive the winter: I have a feeling Felice has found the right spot for it. If so, this will be the first garden in the area to have a flowering azalea next summer. My garden!"

"Your beloved neighbour! There's no denying you were lucky to come across her."

Mrs D. allowed her face to express a deep, unbounded joy:

"You had little opportunity to get to know her, Haakon. That's a pity, although I don't think you would have anything in common, unless I've mis-judged her character. And yours, obviously. Yes, it is a pity, in a sense, but there are some natures one cannot force." After a moment's pause she went on: "You will have a good year in Hamburg. I do hope so. Hamburg is your city now, much more than Bergen. Here nothing ever happens, we're cut off from the world, while Hamburg has everything a man such as yourself could ask for."

Haakon listened, wondering what to make of his mother's words, of her tone of voice. She seemed relieved that he was going: or was this not rather the way triumphant Happiness stoops, generous and aloof, to comfort Defeat? Perhaps she was encouraging him not to ask for anything more. He rose to his feet because once again, as in the hothouse a few hours earlier, he felt as if something were suffocating him. He went out on to the veranda, turning his back on his mother so that she would not see him in this bewildered state.

He decided that the next day, the very next day, he would leave. After all, even his mother quite possibly would not ask why he had brought his departure forward. He devised his plan lucidly. It was not difficult for a single passenger to change reservations, even for the ferry. If necessary he would do without a couchette; as for his packing, he could get that done in less than an hour. He would leave on the usual ten o'clock train from Bergen, but tomorrow, not Sunday. The departure he would so much have liked to postpone must be faced at once. Activity would reassure him, take him out of himself, take him back to the sea, to the long Oslo fjord. In the tranquillity of the crossing he would recover the energy which he was now losing, squandering uselessly in this world of women. He would be regenerated, as if born anew.

He made a sudden move – awkward, like an adolescent. He skipped down the veranda steps and walked towards the stone seat, passing by the azalea and leaving it behind him without so much as a glance in its direction. At the edge of the lake he took off his shoes and socks, rolled up his trouser-legs and ventured a little way into the water. There he stood watching his toes distorted by the reflection of the water, by the ripples arising from the slightest motion, the pumping rhythm of the lake – as on those lazy mornings in the early days, before meeting Felice.

He did not leave on the twelfth. All things considered, he would have been too embarrassed by having to give even the briefest of explanations and by knowing how other people's imaginations would go prying into his motives for going. He left on Sunday morning as arranged – *everything* went as arranged. The taxi (the same one that had met him on his arrival), waited on the drive behind the house, its motor idling. The driver loaded the luggage and Mrs D. ran a gloved finger over the surface of the suitcase, where there was a barely perceptible nick in the leather. The last to get into the car, she asked the driver to close the gate carefully behind them, but not to turn the key.

"Felice will be here soon," Mrs D. explained to Haakon.

Forty minutes were more than enough; the train was precisely on time. Haakon's seat was the furthest from the window; in addition to the pile of newspapers he had just bought, he had a railway timetable, which lay open at the page for the stopping train to Oslo. It would reach Ål station in an hour's time, and ten minutes later there was a bus connection to Torpo, which left from just outside the station. He had roughly an hour's journey ahead of him. He relaxed, leaning back against the velveteen seat, and closed his eyes, covering them with his hand as if the light were troubling him. As he sat thus absorbed in his thoughts, he sensed someone nearby considerately drawing the curtains across the window.

TWENTY-FOUR

MORE OF A VILLAGE than a town, Torpo lay
between mountain and lake, on a strip of land unnamed
even on the road map, and huddled beside the main
road from Ål to Oslo. The bus route ended there: the
vehicle crossed the new bridge, with its low iron spans,
took a wide sweep around the square at the entrance
to the village and came to a halt by a bench, next to
the cemetery gates.

It is always a little embarrassing to be an outsider
arriving in a small town – more so than alighting at
a station in a large city – and Haakon entered Torpo
alone, having been watched with interest by the bus-
driver ever since he had bought his ticket in Ål. The
driver knew of nobody in town who was expecting a
guest or relative on that particular day, so the traveller
aroused his intense curiosity. His passenger left the
bus, suitcase in hand, and, holding out an arm to
counterbalance its weight, walked towards the graveyard fence, towards the two churches, the white one
and the older black one, which stood side by side. Mr
and Mrs D. had been married in the old church, in
the ebony-black building with its small, minutely
storiated door, behind which lay the sepulchre of the
Archbishop of Stavanger.

The graveyard was empty and the church appeared locked up and abandoned, but the door opened when he tried it, revealing an interior which was simply a tall room, its vaulted wooden ceiling decorated with coloured designs. It was bare and empty. Haakon lowered his suitcase to the floor and sat down on a bench by the wall. One could breathe the smell of wood mingled with the damp of centuries, the silence and the gloom. The house by the lake was the same colour as the walls now surrounding him; it had the same sober quality, and Haakon reflected that his mother must have carried the holiness of matrimony away with her to cherish as a secret in the rooms of the house at Bergen.

He looked around for the tomb of Bishop Haakon, where Mr D. had made an offering of his bride's flowers, but there was nothing resembling it anywhere in the church: no memorial-stone, no trace of a grave.

"Over there, right at the foot of the altar, where that mark is carved in the floorboards – that is where the Bishop of Stavanger was buried. He died here in Torpo while he was travelling through Hallingdal and it was his wish to be laid to rest in this church." A young woman, who had entered unobserved, was standing at Haakon's side and recounting – without being asked to – the story of the bishop and his death. There was indeed a rough outline of a human figure. Its head, pointing towards the door, was no more than a semi-circle, while the body was a short tapering cylinder carved into the floorboards.

"They say he did not want any more conspicuous

sign of his passage through this life. But he was a great man, so they say, even though so little trace of him remains." The girl kept her voice low, talking in the slow monotone of someone who is used to saying the same thing time and time again. She was telling a story which the few visitors to the church in Torpo probably knew already and, as she talked, she discreetly offered him a booklet, without asking for money. Haakon took it automatically, turned it over in his hands, then rummaged in his pocket, searching for something – at least a krone – to recompense his guide. He stared over at the faint outline of the tomb and at last saw the place where his father had stood, saw his gesture, the whiteness of his linen suit, the flowers falling on to some arbitrary spot on the floor, now charged with the presence of the long-dead bishop.

Meanwhile the girl had moved away. She must have left the building, because Haakon saw a shaft of light briefly illuminate the floor; then the church was solitary once again. Sitting on the bench with his suitcase by his side, Haakon thought back over the things he had believed he should say to Felice and those he would still like to say. Here, once again, words flowed freely between them, as they had on the mountains above Bergen. They spoke the same language, almost as if their understanding of each other had never ceased, or had been no more broken than a night's sleep interrupts the work and pleasures of waking life. Here he could feel Felice close by him; here he could almost imagine her at his side, motionless, and could relive the act by which, fifty years before, his mother and father had shed lustre on the bare tomb. He saw her nimble fingers wreathing together the flowers.

Haakon's eyes were gradually growing accustomed to the dim light. He rose, walked the length of the short nave to an arch painted with scenes from the life of some saintly woman, looked up and peered through the half-light at the pictures, after which he returned to the bench and picked up the case, which felt heavier than he remembered.

As Haakon went out into the sunlight of the most beautiful nordic afternoon he had ever seen, he noticed the bus parked outside the cemetery gates, a few people already boarding. He made his way towards it slowly, weighed down by the suitcase. When he reached the bus he asked for a ticket to Ål. The driver looked him up and down and recognised his unusual passenger of an hour earlier.

"So you're not staying, sir?"

Haakon shook his head. "I'm going on to Oslo."

"You've got a train in an hour and a half, haven't you?" the driver said. "We'll be there in time, don't worry."

A few minutes later the bus moved off, crossed the bridge and turned right. They reached Ål in perfect time and Haakon, motionless on the platform, saw the train from Bergen appear round the bend, among the crisscrossing railway tracks. He was the only passenger waiting to board, and the train stopped only briefly. It moved off slowly and smoothly, leaving the station behind it, empty.